Turmeric & Sugar

{Stories}

Anna Vangala Jones

Turmeric & Sugar: Stories

Copyright © 2021 Anna Vangala Jones

ISBN-13: 978-1-7345158-7-9

Cover design by Carolyn Brandt

Printed in the U.S.A.

For more titles and inquiries, please visit:

www.thirtywestph.com

Table of Contents

Turmeric & Sugar

Mae and Me

When Daniel vanished, he left two women behind. Mae, our elderly landlady in 4A, and me, his wife. She'd somehow come to have an equal claim on him. We both lost him that day. He'd held Mae's hand as often as mine, each time he led her up the creaking steps to her apartment. Only when Mae and I started to wonder, in a way that ached deep in our bones, if he'd really never return, did she finally have the elevator fixed. She found me a much less suitable companion for the treacherous journey up the stairs.

"Too fast," she'd say. "You act like we're losing in a race, Anjali."

I was impatient, still reeling from Daniel's disappearance. In the absence of any instructions regarding what he would have wanted, I found myself taking care of this unpleasant woman whose company I would have happily avoided—entirely possible in New York City. Before Daniel merged our lives, we were strangers who happened to traverse the same bit of floor. Now the skin on our two bodies seared together with the absence of his fingertips, calloused from guitar strings and rock climbing.

Mae was Daniel's responsibility. I wasn't the one who struck up an acquaintance with our lonely neighbor. We were both teachers, but he'd been laid off from his school due to budget cuts. Daniel began visiting Mae down the hall and grew indispensable to her. Picking up her groceries, staying to throw a haphazard meal together, reading to her as her cataracts worsened, hooking his arm through the crook of her elbow and taking her for slow, meandering walks around our block. He'd tell her, in poetic detail, of his adventures from the world travels that defined him before he became

Mae's voluntary caretaker. She had never left the state.

Their friendship didn't concern me. It gave him something to talk about in bed, as much as stories about Mae bored me. I could tell she gave him purpose. The few times Mae emerged from her lair to come to our door to demand Daniel's help in opening a jar or changing a bulb, we barely acknowledged each other.

Once he was gone, I felt like I should take over and make sure this woman he'd loved would be okay without him.

Besides, focusing my energy on Mae distracted me. It kept me from wondering if Daniel had been taken from me or wandered away of his own volition. Still, even as we talked over tea or listened to her blaring television while I prepared dinners soft enough for her new dentures, Daniel's low voice whispered doubts in my ear.

"Have the police found anything new?" she asked one night, her loud voice drowning out the contestant's correct response on Jeopardy.

I shifted uncomfortably, like I did whenever she brought up my missing husband. "I was watching that. Now I don't know the answer."

"You can Google it later." Ever since Daniel had taught Mae how to use Google, it was her solution to everything. "No updates?"

They had scanned each security tape in the vicinity of Mae's brownstone and leading up to the entrances of nearby Central Park, then all the ones close to every bridge in the city. They scoured the Hudson many times over, weeks apart. His body would have floated to the surface by now, Detective Wilson had explained. His more tactful partner reassured us that it must mean Daniel was alive, wherever he was. I still couldn't decide which was better.

**

I had to call and tell his mother whom he hadn't spoken to in years and had only introduced me to once. Daniel's father had left when she was pregnant. Needy and demanding Daniel's constant attention and affection, she rained down verbal acid whenever Daniel couldn't give her all she wanted and craved from the man who'd abandoned them.

"Always knew he'd pull something like this," his mother said. "Selfish. Gone and left you just like his dad did to me. Lucky you don't have any kids." Her triumphant I-told-you-so inflection was unbearable. I wanted to slap her, not just for her heartless and cold attitude now, but for the years he'd suffered as her child.

It was during his adolescent years that he'd first experimented with cutting himself and his substance abuse problems began. Daniel said he couldn't go to his mother for help because she treated him like a disturbed monster lurking in her home. By the time I met him, he was a gentle, thoughtful history teacher who had scaled mountains on almost every continent.

"He didn't pull anything," I said. "He started getting depressed again after he got laid off. I thought he was doing better after a while, but he wasn't. He's gone, and you should care because you're his mother."

Her long silence on the other end chilled me from my hairline to my toes. Just when I thought she must have hung up, she cleared her throat. "Oh, sweetie. He did a real number on you. Trust me, you're better off."

**

Mae started peeking out her door every time she heard me opening mine after work. Sometimes I told her I was too tired to join her, but eventually I was over there more days than I wasn't.

Soon, Mae began rattling off vignettes of her life's story, like I was her willing biographer. I came to depend on her tales for relief from my anxiety about Daniel. My fear for him consumed me the rest of the time.

Sometimes I wondered if Mae invented it all. But that would be too beneath her. Mae's pride wouldn't allow her to lie about her glittering and gritty life as a Broadway dancer and her torrid love affair with the director. Embellishment of the details seemed more likely.

"They auditioned hundreds of gals for the part," she said one time after dinner, "but once I sashayed into that room, Reggie couldn't remember a single one of them. He couldn't remember his wife the longer he watched me dance."

I tried not to be judgmental, though I knew she wanted me to be, a little bit at least. If I was too accepting of her greatest misdeed and normalized it too much, then her existence lost all its spice, her love all its heady flavor. She counted on that past excitement of their wrongdoing to keep her interesting now, as she and her director had gone on to spend a perfectly boring and happy life together after their affair ended his first marriage. He was Mae's husband for forty-seven years until his death, and the children they never had, left her all alone.

"You and Daniel never faced any obstacles to you being together," Mae said, waving her hand as she saw me gearing up to protest. "Oh, I know, you were brown, he was white, what would your parents think, and all that jazz—but you kids can do most things you want just fine now. You tell everyone where to shove it and then you shack up together." She waited. I didn't interrupt. "Very little can stand in your way. Reggie and me—"

Mae's voice trailed off as she fingered a nearby framed photograph of them on their wedding day, like she forgot I was in the room. It was black and white, and Mae was laughing in it, gazing up at her husband in a way I never had at Daniel. Daniel made me burn with heat when he held me close, but it wasn't often that he made me laugh.

"Mae?"

"What?" She looked confused, and I knew it was getting late.

"Reggie and you. You were talking about obstacles. How you had to walk twenty miles in the snow to get to Reggie and build the chapel yourselves before you could get married."

"Oh, very funny, Miss. I'm old and you've heard it all before. Why don't you blow it out your ass, wise guy." Mae shoved my shoulder hard with an unexpected strength that made me smile in spite of myself.

I started to stand but felt her staring. I was startled by the way she leaned back and spread her arms, baring herself to me like she was naked.

"Reggie made me love him more than the stage, and I didn't think anyone ever could. It didn't matter that we were different religions, or that he was older and accomplished, and I was just some sassy kid with long legs and feet that wouldn't stay still. No, Miss, there was a twister picking up speed all around us from the moment I walked into that room and he asked my name." She shrugged. "No wife of his stood a chance."

It was when she would get into the sordid particulars, like the time they made love in his director's chair backstage with the rest of the cast and crew dangerously nearby, that I'd squint and scrunch my nose in disbelief. But as Mae would tell me whenever she detected skepticism, "What do I care about impressing you? Who are you, sweetheart?" Or "You think I'd spend the precious time I have left dreaming up stories to show off for you? Polishing them up before you get here?" Always followed by a defensive snort, as if she, too, began to question the reality of her own history's retelling.

**

I had been the first to meet Mae, not Daniel. I'd applied for the apartment when he was still only my boyfriend, so I didn't bring him along when I went to go see 4B.

When I arrived at the foot of a majestic looking, bird shit stained staircase, an old woman sat in a rocking chair on the landing, yawning. A fly buzzed around both our heads as I walked up to meet her. She swatted it away from a cheek caked in the blood red rouge of an earlier time. Flyaway wisps of snow-colored hair, sprinkled with traces of the rich brunette it once was, framed her heavily lined face. A few strands clung to her forehead, damp with sweat. Her eyes, a steely gray, stared off into nothing.

"Glad you're a teacher," she said, grunting as I helped her up out of the chair. We'd chatted on the phone a day earlier. "Means you'll be quiet—grading and lesson planning, and whatnot." She pushed her glasses back to the bridge of her nose and peered at my features more closely. "Not wearing makeup. You Indian women are modest folk—that's good, too." Her back was to me as she placed her key in the lock and said, "Not that it seems likely, but any obnoxious music or loud sex and I'll have your ass back out on the street."

The building was hot and stuffy when she took me inside. Mae claimed the air conditioner was running, but the oppressive stillness of the heat in the unit was inescapable. It also reeked of Mae's cigarette smoke, which would go on to curl and wisp out of my vents at all hours once I moved in. She and I gazed around at the small space, pretending together that there was anything more to tour than the room we were standing in already. The fact that I'd be able to reach out and touch the microwave from my bed was not an appealing prospect.

But I was charmed by the rust red and tan color of the old, dusty bricks stretching from floor to high ceiling. This Upper West Side recluse's haven was also steps from Central Park in the genuine way, not the Craigslist false promises followed by a dozen exclamation points way. It was ideal for my early morning runs with Daniel before the school bells started ringing in our ears and jostling our brains all day. Mae could see all this in my eyes and sensed the hard sell wouldn't be necessary.

"Well, go on. Take a look around without me hovering, but hurry up."

**

The two years following Daniel's disappearance stretched on like a decade. He still haunted every inch of the tiny studio, and any time I caught myself feeling vain and smiling at my appearance in the mirror, he stared back at me from behind the glass, wondering with his hurt expression who I was trying to look pretty for with his fate still unknown. The neighborhood search parties had long since dispersed, his photo was no longer being shared on Facebook, and my colleagues and students couldn't decide whether to treat me like a widow or divorcee.

An old classmate from my high school, Rohan, reached out to me. He was new to the city and didn't know anyone. As dinner with him approached, little things like the choice of romantic restaurant and his increasingly flirtatious texts made it start to seem like this was more of a date than a friendly reunion. In many ways, it felt too soon. But Mae didn't think so.

"You being a shut in and not getting any won't bring Daniel back," she said. Her frankness and embrace of modern speak helped me to loosen up. "And you've never dated one of your own kind, have you?"

I shook my head, ignoring her rude phrasing. Growing up in rural Connecticut hadn't led to interaction with many other Indians.

"Well, I say go and get a free meal." She looked me up and down, like she was surveying a beat up car in need of a wash and paint job. "Maybe a trip to the salon first."

Mae's encouragement somehow felt more important than that of my friends, like if she thought it was okay for me to take a break from my bleak Friday night routine of wine and Netflix alone in Daniel's old T-shirt, then it wasn't as disloyal to him as I knew it was.

**

Rohan and I were dating before I realized it. Six months with him rushed by. He made me laugh. We rediscovered the city that I'd once loved before it became such a lonely, foreign place without Daniel. We walked the length of the Brooklyn Bridge. We pretended to appreciate an art exhibit at the MOMA made up entirely of text messages, including messy break-up ones. We ate soup dumplings at Shanghai Joe's in Chinatown and Shake Shack burgers all over the city. We were so busy being tourons, as Daniel would have called us (tourist and moron rolled into one), that my apartment at night was the only place left where I was forced to remember I was a missing man's wife.

It was on a hike in the Adirondacks that Rohan asked me a serious question I wasn't anticipating. That night, I dropped by Mae's for dinner.

When I let myself in and joined her at the kitchen table, Mae was fanning herself with her checkbook. I started to ramble about how humid it was.

"Save it," Mae said. "I can tell you've got something on your mind."

I was relieved. I didn't have to build my way up to what was weighing on me. "Rohan wants to move in together."

Mae stared at me, like she was the teacher and I was her student, searching for the right answer in her eyes.

"It's too fast," I said.

"You seem to really like him, Anjali."

"I know I do. But something's not right. I need to end it."

Mae's impassive face caught me off guard. I'd never had trouble reading it before. "Before you do that, there's something I need to tell you."

Her tone of voice made my shoulders tense.

"It's about Daniel."

The world stopped turning for an instant and my memory of how to keep breathing did, too. "What are you talking about? Daniel? Has he tried to contact you—"

Mae started clicking her teeth and shushing me in a lilting rhythm, like I was a baby jolted out of a deep sleep that she needed to rock back into dreaming. "No, no, nothing like that." She sat up straighter. "You know his mom put Daniel's grandmother in a home once the dementia overtook her and she required constant care? He wanted her to come live with them, but his mother said it would be too hard. Probably would have been."

"He told me his grandma was dead," I said, breathing steadily again. I was pretty sure Mae was confusing him for someone else. Daniel had mentioned she was getting more easily mixed up as their time together progressed.

"And she was, by the time he met you." She sounded too confident to be wrong, but Mae was always confident.

"I don't get what this has to do with—"

"He was closer to his grandmother than anyone," Mae said. "She was the only one that he could talk to about the darkness. The sadness. How he couldn't control it anymore. How it always came back."

"I didn't know that," I said, the hurt flaring in my belly and ricocheting like a firecracker. "How could he not tell me any of that?"

"I imagine as young people falling in love, you were often busy doing other things," Mae said, her eyebrow arched and her smile mischievous. Then it disappeared. "But when he started to get that drowning feeling again, all he could think of that might help to pull him back above water was her. So he turned to me."

I was embarrassed by the wetness pricking at my eyes and refused to let them develop into tears in front of Mae. "So he couldn't even talk to me." I looked at the floor instead of her.

"Wait, Anjali. I'm trying to tell you something."

I motioned for her to continue.

"He'd started using again. The drugs. A lot."

I snapped back to attention. "What drugs? Which ones? He said he'd never—"

Mae cut me off with the usual wave of her hand. "Not really the point, is it? Better you don't know. But that's why he was over here so much. Didn't want you to see him like that." She waited for me to respond, but I didn't. "It got so bad that he showed up to work one morning, just gone out of his mind, trying to teach the kids. They fired him on the spot." She cleared her throat. "That's what really happened. No budget cuts. No layoffs. It nearly killed him, and he didn't want you to know."

One punch in the stomach after another stops feeling like anything, after a while. You just go numb and still, hoping it'll be over soon.

"Is that all?" I asked.

Mae nodded.

"I never really knew him, did I? I didn't try hard enough. I didn't make him happy."

"That's not anything you did wrong. You were what he needed in other ways. There's no accounting for what comforts a person once they're in that state." Her rough voice was smooth and thick now, warming me from the inside like steaming hot chocolate. "You couldn't fix him, honey. Neither could I. That'd be like blaming ourselves if we couldn't cure someone's cancer. Your husband was sick, and he was always doing the best he could."

In a rare moment of physical connection between us, I felt her hand— all wrinkles, blue veins, and bones—resting on my head. I glanced up to find her standing beside me.

"You and I did the best we could, too," she said. "He loved us and we loved him. I don't know what happened to him or where he is, but I do know that."

I tried to nod, but when I crumbled forward into her thin, weathered arms, they were ready for me. Close enough to inhale the scent of her menthols and brassy perfume, a memory sprang to my mind, one so insignificant I didn't even know it was buried there.

It was early evening on a sultry day. I'd been out afternoon drinking with some friends as we often did in the summer months. Daniel had said he wanted to stay in to read a book. I stumbled into our studio with laughter on my lips only to find the place empty. Irritated that the funny story I was excited to tell him would be forgotten, I went looking for him at Mae's. I never had before. When I rapped on the door, I'm sure I must have startled them.

Yet they didn't change positions to stand up and come let me in. It's open, Mae had called out, boredom in her tone. When I entered, neither looked up. They were on the gray loveseat. Mae was seated upright—but Daniel was curled up like a spoon, his head in her lap, her blue-veined fingers combing his golden curls. I stared for a second before glancing over at the television to see what they were watching. It was off.

Was that the day he told Mae the truth he couldn't tell me? With his soft hair pressed against her sharp pelvic bone in the smoky haze of her musty smelling apartment—the very picture of intimacy.

Suddenly, I felt sick. I extricated myself from Mae's warmth, stood up, and walked out her front door without another word.

**

Once all my things were stowed in the back of the U-Haul, Rohan climbed into the driver seat.

I turned and made my way back up the staircase to Mae. She was waiting for me. Above her was the home and ghost of a husband I had to leave behind to be able to start living again. I felt awful that it meant I needed to leave Mae, too. She was so tightly and inextricably wound up in my uncertain lingering need for Daniel, as well as the pain and anger his memory inspired, that I couldn't keep going with her the way things had been. As the women who had lived with, loved, and mourned Daniel together, I couldn't take her with me or return to her with any great frequency. It would be like staying married to Daniel while trying to make a fresh beginning with Rohan.

"This is just a see you later," I said. But something of my guilt and hesitance seeped out of my pores, because Mae fixed me with a long look, her nostrils flaring.

"You take care, Anjali." Set against the background of the looming sturdy brownstone, she looked smaller and frailer than usual.

**

The following spring, nearly nine months later, I was at the front of my classroom when my cell phone rang. I never answer during a lesson, so I let it go to voicemail. The bell rang, and as my students spilled out into the hallway, I glanced at the phone. My stomach lurched when the screen lit up again. It was Detective Wilson. We rushed through the polite hellos.

"We recovered a body from the river." My hearing dissolved into nothing. I could tell he was still talking, but I missed it. "Anjali? Are you there?"

"Yes."

"Did you hear what I just said?"

"No."

"The remains were unrecognizable as any person, so we ran it against Daniel's dental records."

I leaned forward. "And?"

"It's not him. All our other leads have already gone cold. Every person that's called to report someone that looks like him, that could be him, they've been wrong."

"What's next?"

"They're reassigning me to another case."

"I don't understand. Who will be taking on Daniel's?"

He sighed. "Sometimes, people leave, Anjali. They just run." For a second, the face of Daniel's mother smirking was all I could see, but I blinked and she was gone. "I really am sorry."

**

When I got home, Rohan was still at work. I gravitated to my side of the shared closet in our bedroom. I had to use a stepladder to reach the purple shoebox I kept wedged in the corner of the shelf on top. It's where I stored the few of Daniel's things I took with me when I moved. The rest I had left with Mae or donated to Goodwill.

I rubbed Daniel's guitar pick with a light pressure at first. It was red with white marbling, like raw meat. I pressed it harder against my fingers, leaving an indent in my skin, like it would make me feel something. Like I'd suddenly know what happened to him and hear him tell me that he's okay. Hear him tell me why he left. I closed my eyes and placed it against my forehead, trying to listen for him. It was as cold and inflexible as glass.

I waited for the feel of his sandpaper hands to sweep my coarse hair aside and caress my shoulders, for his lips to whisper along the nape of my neck. There was only one person that could ever help me to connect with Daniel again, and I walked away from her. I hadn't even returned to the intersection or the stretch of uneven sidewalk that would put me in too close range of the brownstone I called home for years.

The truth burned in my chest—that Mae had been taking care of me for him, more than the other way around. I returned the shoebox to its place and headed outside to the subway station.

**

I got buzzed up without a word and wondered for a moment if it was really her letting me in. Afraid of who I might or might not find up there, I paced in the entryway for a bit. Then I avoided the rickety elevator and started climbing the many familiar steps. As I neared the fourth floor, I coughed and noticed the layer of dust beneath my palm on the mahogany banister. I dragged my hand across my skirt, marking myself with the evidence of my neglect. When I knocked, it felt like an eternity before the door finally eased open.

Looking at her for the first time in so long, I felt like an ashamed kid in the corner after my time-out. Contrite, with hands behind my back and dragging my feet. "Hey, Mae."

She leaned hard on her walking cane, her gray eyes blurry behind her thick lenses but penetrating my soul anyway. I don't know why I expected her to age dramatically since I'd last seen or spoken to her, but she didn't look too different. I realized that the warmth making my fingers and toes tingle was from the relief surging through me that she wasn't already dead.

"I'm sorry it's been a while," I said.

"Yes. But I'm glad you came." Mae, to my grateful surprise, didn't prolong this introduction to our awkward reunion. She turned and shuffled away, leaving me alone in the doorway. "Tea's almost ready."

A framed photo of a plaintive Daniel on the wall, beside one of her and Reggie, gave me pause. But it didn't hurt exactly. I smiled and followed.

You Don't Have a Place Here

I have a scheduled meeting today with Caroline, our team's HR rep, and I'm glad you'll be coming with me so I don't have to be alone with her. There's something cold about her I don't like. She's nice, sure. Just feels like the air conditioning is cranked up too high when she's around.

Caroline isn't the small talk type, so I'm not worried by her brusque "Let's get started, shall we?" as soon as I'm seated across from her. Not too sure what this could be about, but I'm a decent employee, so can't be anything serious.

"Starting sounds good to me." I smile, but she's not looking at me.

I'm surprised when she tells me that it's you she wants to talk about, not me. The issue is you're not supposed to be here, it sounds like.

She says you make people around the office feel uneasy.

"How so?" I want to know, but ask polite as can be. I'm offended, of course, but best not to get defensive.

The first time I sensed you were still nearby and not as gone as we'd all assumed was on the Wednesday after the funeral. One of the cherry tomatoes I was about to mix into my salad rolled itself right off the counter, and I didn't realize in time to miss stepping on it and splattering emerald green juice and seeds everywhere. You were forever dropping grapes and cherry tomatoes, you remember. Your grip on everything was tenuous, your touch too light and gentle. It made me wonder. I was relieved the more I felt you around, the more sure I became. Our apartment would be too big and much messier without you in it. I never wanted to live in the city without my roommate.

So many people whispered into my hair and left my neck damp and gritty with the salt of their tears in the chaotic hours after you were first found. A body, the police officer called you.

"She didn't even like you that much," I said to one of your acquaintances who cried the loudest, but it's probably for the best she didn't hear me. She'll only miss you until she doesn't anymore anyway.

I'm pretty sure you stay because I want you to. What I mean is you don't hang around to punish me or anything. Best friends since I asked to borrow your neon pink glitter pen in fourth grade. I don't feel afraid or even sad that you're still here. I'd be both those things if you left. I think you know that, too. I feel bad I was your burden before and you're still not free of carrying me around on your shoulders now.

Caroline is answering me, so I try to pay better attention. "I mean, you walk around here making it uncomfortably clear to all of us that the specter is there beside you. Following you around. For everything. Everywhere you go." She stares like my face will change to indicate that I agree with what she's telling me, but she's going to be waiting a long time if she thinks that will happen. Since I don't pipe up with what's expected of me, she shuffles the stack of pages in her lap expertly, like a dealer with a deck of cards. "It's strange," she says. "To put it mildly."

"The mild version is hot enough." I follow this up with a too loud awkward laugh that I can still hear even after my mouth is closed again.

She doesn't smile. "The specter cannot join us here at work anymore, I'm afraid." Her voice is smooth and kind enough. Word choice delicate. But she is firm. "You'll just have to leave that kind of personal baggage at home. It doesn't have a place here."

"Specter. Is that a word people even use anymore?" I say, my cheerful tone not doing enough to mask the hurt straining to burst free and roam wild around the office. Peeking into people's cubicles, demanding to know who has complained about you to HR, about us. Because you're such a part of me that you and I know it's both of us they must have a problem with, not one or the other. We're too intertwined now for that to even work.

She looks up and nods. "That's the word they use here in the paperwork. Would you like to see?"

"No. I trust you."

When I get back to my desk, one of my coworkers whose name is Joy with a personality to match is there, sitting on it. I try to pretend she isn't and drop into my chair and swivel it away from her to face my computer.

"Caroline told you, huh?"

"About your formal complaint?" I say, willing the bright screen of my computer to shatter and rain glass shards all over Joy and everyone else, too. I picture it wedge and burrow its way deep into their skin—eyes electrified by the shock of pain—and for a second, I'm happy again, like before the meeting.

"Well, it wasn't just me," Joy says, hopping off my desk. She doesn't leave though. "I'm sorry it hurts your feelings," she adds, and I can tell she means it. I am grateful for her checking in with me, but I'd much rather be alone with you right now. "That's why it's taken so long for anyone to even say anything to Caroline. We understand how hard this has been for you. No one's wanted to rush your—you know—process. However long you need to move on."

Now I'm okay with letting her know I'm a little annoyed. "Move on? That's rude. You don't get it. She didn't leave. So I don't have to move on." My air quotes are a bit exaggerated, and my words vibrate with too much sarcasm and irritation for her to ignore.

"I shouldn't have said that then. Unfair for me to presume. You're right. Sorry."

Joy doesn't seem to bother you as much as she does me. But you are the mellow, generous one out of us two. The roommate who does all the dishes if I've left mine to soak and throws my laundry in with yours without so much as a passive aggressive grunt or eye roll. You haven't changed much since the fourth grade in that way. I've grown a little. Stopped taking advantage of your kindness as much by our late teens. The leaning on you, though, letting your love prop me up—I still haven't shaken those habits yet.

Joy's been talking, but I'm pretty confident I haven't missed anything important. I catch the end. "I've talked to my therapist about your situation—how you bring her to work with you every day—and he says it's probably you trying to cope with your surv—"

"No. It's not that." I cut her off. She doesn't need to finish. We don't need to hear the rest. You and I have both heard of survivor's guilt before. We're not idiots.

Sometimes we reenact that night together. We go through the steps, you and me, like parts we've memorized in a too familiar play that stars only us two. It always starts the same way. At the bar. I want to get going. You're having fun.

"When you want to stay out longer and I want to go home, I don't leave you," you tell me. Your fingers on my arm are too timid. Perhaps you should grip me harder so I won't leave you. What you say is true, but it doesn't matter. I'm tired and anxious and I don't want to be here anymore. In my mind I've already left. We both order rides home two hours apart on the same app. Mine drops me off at our apartment. Yours never does.

"What was she like?" Joy asks now.

"What's she like?" I shake my head and gesture at you.

Joy doesn't say anything. Just waits. Patient, quiet, unruffled. She reminds me of you, but only for a moment. "She's really nice." I stare at you instead of her, and that's how I can say it without dissolving right here in the middle of this stupid office. This lonely place full of people who don't want you here. Who don't understand it means they don't want me here either. Not sure why it bothers me when I don't even want to be here.

"I bet. Want to go down the street to the deli? Eat lunch there today maybe?" Joy half smiles. "I won't talk. If you'd prefer."

"Yeah, okay." My purse is already in my hands, even though I can't tell you how it got there. Maybe you should tell me. I motion for you to come with us, and I dare Joy to report me to HR. Wish she would, I tell you. You don't seem to be listening though. I'm not sure you hear me.

A Day for Watching Birds

Her shoes aren't ones she chose to walk in, but they're the shoes she's been given. They're brown and scuffed and the laces have that frayed, gray, been in too many puddles look to them. Shabby. His glasses are bigger than his head, and he's better at trivia than whoever it was that made up the questions.

Mira and Ravi are sixteen years old when they first meet. He lives in a top floor apartment on a loud street in Queens. It's a frosty day, and the tree outside his bedroom window is bare. The branches are more like angry arms with jagged, pointy fingertips, but the sky there is forever periwinkle blue. Mira happens to be passing by and stops to look up.

European starlings are perched atop the tree's twigs. They are a boring brown with some white spots instead of their summer plumage of iridescent black with purples and greens, but Mira doesn't mind. She hears their singing and whistling cut through the sky with pleasure. She lifts the binoculars she constantly keeps on her person for just such an occasion.

Ravi yanks his window up and leans all the way out of it to shout, "Are those actual binoculars, you sick perv?"

Mira flips him the finger. "Get over yourself."

His face flutters and blooms into a smile. He motions for her to come join him.

For a time, they aren't alone anymore. After his bookshelf that holds both Vonnegut and Amelia Bedelia, their togetherness is what she likes best about him. Ravi likes the wonder that only he can see beaming out of her quiet eyes when she reads passages of her chemistry textbook aloud to him. When they hold hands, skin against skin, they're brown and beautiful and nothing can hurt them. The globe outside their birdcage doesn't exist, not until it's time to pry themselves apart.

They were in love up there for a little while before they weren't.

Whenever she finds herself below that window again, she tells herself it's to watch the birds. There are always two of them, and their necks are intertwined until the music they're making becomes one song.

When he sees her down there, he tips his imaginary hat to her. Then he looks out to the branches, level with his world shaped eyes, and they watch the birds together.

Echo

Before she was a girl, she'd been an elephant. She wasn't supposed to remember that, but somewhere in the reincarnation system there'd been a glitch. Her memory had come with her. Now nothing in this life could satisfy, as she had a whole other one to forever measure it against. When she was an elephant, she remembered longing to be a girl, as they seemed to have things better overall. Now, after an excruciating stretch in this human body, she wasn't so sure. The past held a promise of a better future, but this present seemed eternal and fixed.

It had been a hunter and his hunger for ivory that ended her life as an elephant. Now it was a man and his greed for her body that made her life as a girl just as precarious and intolerable. What she'd done to deserve male lust stalking her as prey across two lifetimes, she was sure she didn't know. She was determined now that the ending would not remain the same.

She wouldn't be conquered, she wouldn't be owned, and sold in parts—not when given a second chance. Her soul had stayed intact for a purpose. Freedom lingered just beyond the barred windows of her current cage, a shed in the man's backyard, so like the one her elephant body had inhabited after it shuddered its last breaths and collapsed with seeming finality upon the dusty earth.

Her skin, a cracked and rough gray, was now a smooth and soft brown. Yielding yet resilient, like tightly coiled springs.

The hunter had not allowed for a fair fight. He'd followed her first in his jeep, built for the terrain, and then on foot. He stalked her for some time from a distance before positioning his rifle just so and aiming for her wide, unprotected back as she bathed herself. She remembered the quiet. She remembered the peace. She wondered how long he watched her before firing the shot that brought a life full of beautiful possibilities to an abrupt end. If he'd contemplated what all came before that moment for her and what all could have come after had he changed his mind; if he spared even a sliver of thought for how she deserved to live and flourish for herself rather than die and be used for his pleasure. The feeling of the bullet penetrating her, the burning and tearing sensations, the slow agony, the merciless pressure, the shock building into horror, the pain, the fear—it had come coursing back through her every nerve ending that first night in the man's shed. His ugly face looming in the darkness, the weight of his knees, the stench of his hot breath so close, the terror of today's brutal reality, and the fear of tomorrows with no hope.

She'd been on a bus with her high school debate team when the man began following them—first in his car and then on foot at the gas station rest stop. She'd never forget the music that played that day, now echoing for eternity—the explicit lyrics, the pounding bass, the cacophony of her classmates' voices singing along—imprinted upon her soul as the last moments of her freedom and innocence. Just like the man's fingerprints were now tattooed into her flesh as the enduring bruises of her imprisonment and all he'd taken from her since.

But today, as he stumbled into her shed, he was intoxicated, and she could smell weakness on him. Vulnerability intermingled with bourbon emanated from his pores. His foot caught on a crooked plank that he usually knew to sidestep, and he tripped. It was now or never.

She reared back and charged at his fallen figure with terrifying speed, the hardest part of her skull focused on the point between his eyes and her nails outstretched and curled, ready to pierce his flesh. She'd been attacked from behind last time so her curved sharp tusks had been useless as weapons and were preserved instead as the hunter's prize. This time, the man would know defeat. She felt a drunken rush of power surge through her when his face contorted in fear at her fast approach.

There was nothing very intimidating about her slight frame. She was slender with a doughy tummy, all pointy knees and elbows where her skin was the darkest brown and dry like puckered raisins. But there was no time to concern herself with how he could be afraid of a girl like her. She rammed her head into his, and his eyes rolled back. She reversed and stampeded him again. Her strength swelled as he lay crumpled flat on the ground. She could feel ribs and bones cracking beneath her tremendous feet as she trampled and stomped with a delight she hadn't felt in years.

It was only then that she caught her reflection in the small dirt splattered mirror above him. She was enormous and gray, her ears billowing around her head like sails in a warm breeze.

She coiled him up in her trunk, lifting and slamming his near lifeless body to the ground. Over and over she did it, to be certain. She released him more out of curiosity than anything and waited. As he staggered up to meet her, the look in his eyes as wild and frenzied as it was afraid and hopeless, she allowed her tusks the victory they'd been denied before. Dark red, almost purple, flecks of him freckled her gray shell, but she plowed on. She watched the man shudder his last breaths as his body collapsed to the earth below him. A translucent, dark puddle of his blood formed around him, sparkling with his sweat like diamonds.

She trotted out into the sunlight, letting it bathe and bake her tired armor. As she settled herself in a position comfortable enough for rest, she raised her majestic head and looked all around her for any potential predators. Reborn, she closed her eyes and slept.

Summer Love

Annika has fallen in love. Annika is a bit bedraggled looking if all she receives is a quick distracted glance. If allowed time to contemplate her, though, looking at her face is all anyone would want to do. Pain, beauty, and wonder wound up tight in a deceptively boring package. Annika thinks it's better not to be noticed, but now she'd give anything to be seen and found appealing by this one person. But each day at school, the love of Annika's life glides away as Annika trails behind, quiet but alert. They don't smile at each other, but Annika has caught a mutual glance here and there. It's hard to say why the two never connect as time goes whooshing past.

Her name is Summer. She's a senior and Annika is a sophomore. Annika can sometimes be found just below Summer's bedroom window, having paused there on her own way home—at first it was infrequent, then about once a month, until it became an almost weekly occurrence. Summer and her visitors are often high together on her bed, moving to the rhythm of The Beatles blasting over the stereo. When they feel like being cool, they play The Beatles. When they feel like indulging in the pride of being predictable, they play Hanson. No one mmm bops better than Annika's love.

Annika thinks Summer is a beautiful songbird. One that is meant to be admired, but not up close. Most days, she just watches Summer go about her routine. Preening herself in front of the mirror. Clashing with her mother in a volume so loud that all the birds in the vicinity fly for cover. Reading a magazine with music blasting and drowning out her thoughts.

Summer's father often comes in to yell at her to turn it down. She is unflappable. She gets up from her bed without a word, slams the door in his face, puts on enormous headphones, perfect for blocking out the sounds of the unwelcome world around her, and dances with a wild energy. Annika hopes that someday Summer will be free.

**

"What are you doing?"

Annika is startled by Summer's melodious tones behind her as she is caught staring up into her empty bedroom one afternoon, waiting for her. Annika drops into an unsettling crouched position, as though there is a bush she's hiding behind, but she's out in plain sight.

"Oh," Summer says. "It's you, you weirdo. You know, I've seen you watching me. At school. Here. What's the matter with you anyway? Do you even live around here?"

Annika's throat and mouth are dry and cracking into a thousand shattered shards. Her love is speaking to her! Her love wants to learn more about her! She forgets to answer her.

"What, are you slow or something?"

"No," she says and stands up. "I'm Annika."

Summer laughs. Annika doesn't dare look away from her love's mouth. Her lips are cranberry colored.

"Okay, Annika. Well, you look lonely and hungry and like you could use a friend or a hit of something. C'mon in." She leads a spellbound Annika into the rundown apartment building she calls home. To Annika, it's a grand palace to which she's been granted unexpected entry. It's a fourth floor walk-up, so she follows the sound of Summer humming a familiar tune all the way up the stairs, not pausing her rapt attention for even a second. She fears that if her love stops singing, or if Annika stops listening, the magic will be over and she'll wake up back outside and alone.

Once inside the long watched bedroom, Summer offers her a joint and some Wheat Thins. They sit on the twin bed and pass it back and forth as they smoke together for the first and last time. They don't talk much during this brief visit. Summer mostly comments on how strange Annika is, but how she seems sweet enough and it's hard not to feel sorry for her. "You shouldn't just hang around outside people's windows, you know. It's creepy as fuck." She takes a hit and coughs out her continuing stream of thoughts. "But you seem harmless. You've got kind eyes, I think. I mostly just feel depressed as shit when I see you out there, always alone." Annika is silent but tries to be charming with too eager nods and smiles at the end of every statement her love utters. At one point, without awareness of what she is doing, Annika reaches out and strokes Summer's hair while she is busy gazing out the window, stoned, and doesn't see Annika coming in time to stop her.

Summer rears back. Annika knows she's spooked her. Better to watch. Never ever touch. "Well, that's done anyway." Summer grinds the crinkled, blackened, rolled-up paper into an ashtray and then goes to flush it down the toilet in the bathroom at the end of the narrow hallway. When she returns, she stares at Annika until she realizes it's time for her to leave.

Summer gave her a chance, and Annika blew it. It's awkward and painful to spend the precious minutes and hours of a finite life spying on someone who doesn't want you anymore. Annika is embarrassed to be banished back to her old position outside the building, but she can't go home either. It's hard to hide from Annika's parents and their constant arguing there. There's also no Summer.

**

Summer seems to have written off the incident as some *oh, we were just high and she's socially awkward* thing, but she doesn't invite Annika up again. Annika is pretty sure she's invisible to her most of the time, but once or twice she thinks that Summer notices that Annika is still out there, watching and waiting. Otherwise, Summer continues on with her life as it was before the interruption—the unremarkable blip—that was Annika's visit.

A few weeks pass, and one day Annika is kept waiting longer than usual. Her love should be getting home any minute. She hears her musical laughter and is startled when it's followed by a deep male voice. They round the corner and enter Annika's line of sight. He is tall with brown hair coated in gel. His pants sag too low, and he's got an impertinent arm around Summer's shoulders. He's not from their school. Annika might be growling and baring her teeth, but she isn't sure. He walks Summer home to the propped open door of the reddish-brown building, and they stay there a while. Summer is leaning back against the doorframe, her breasts and hips thrust up and out in a clearly primal stance that Annika is uncomfortable to witness. He has his arm extended over her head, his hand pressed against the doorframe, as he leans in over her. He's looking down at her. She's looking up at him. Their voices grow softer. Annika wishes she could be happy for them, if Summer is happy.

Annika passes Summer's apartment building without stopping for a couple months after that day. Summer has chosen him. Continuing to watch can only bring Annika pain. She spends most of her time at the library to evade the reality of her parents' impending divorce. She throws herself back into books which is where all her concentration had been focused before Summer, but it doesn't work. It's July now, so she can't catch glimpses of her at school anymore. She's reminded how lonely she was before falling in love. She returns to her post, knowing that to truly love with devotion, it can't matter whether it's given in kind. Her love for Summer is determined and unyielding like a river, satisfied to flow in one direction.

Sometimes Summer and the boyfriend fight. He's not as loud as her, but he curses a lot. When he really gets going, there's barely any clean language to be excavated from the rubble of the tirade. Summer knows how to infuriate him when he is like this. She fixes him with her bored stare and then flutters about the room, tidying up like she can't hear him, like he isn't even there.

On the day that he is the most upset she's ever seen him, Annika observes him gesticulating and hears unkind words float down from the window. Summer's tactic of casually ignoring him is too much for him to bear this time. He grabs her by the wrist and yanks her to his chest. Then he's got her by the shoulders and he's shaking her and shaking her, as though he can make the words and emotions she's withholding come spilling out against her will. Summer breaks free, and with a sound that echoes through the neighborhood, she slaps him across the face. Now he's throwing her down on the bed and climbing over her. His long back is blocking Annika's view. Annika knows she is there for watching, not interfering, but this is her love. She is rare. Annika has to save her.

Annika runs to his car in the parking lot—a beat up old orange Impala—and looks around for a weapon. She sees a stray plank of wood on a nearby patch of grass. She's picking it up and swinging it at the driver side window with all her might. There is glass everywhere. She hears the sounds of their arguing stop, and she ducks down to lay flat on the blacktop.

"What the hell? My car, baby, someone's stealing my car!"

"Oh my god, well, hurry up and go stop him!"

His face disappears from the window and Annika knows she has a mere minute to get away. As she flees the scene, she glances back over her shoulder to see Summer, with her elbows on the windowsill, staring back at her. She whispers, "Go away, Annika, and don't come back."

**

On a too hot Sunday morning, Summer and her parents are loading her things into the trunk of the boyfriend's car. There's shiny duct tape on the window. She turned nineteen a week earlier. The summer months are drawing to a close. She is going away to college on a scholarship. He is going to drive the four of them there to help her move into the dorms. Annika has heard the term "heartbreak" before, but never has its meaning been so literal. She watches as he and Summer's parents head back inside for the last of the boxes.

Summer remains behind alone and turns, looking around uncomfortably. She knows she is being watched. "Come out, Annika. Stop fucking with me. I know you're here somewhere."

Annika emerges and approaches, careful and cautious.

"What do you want?" Summer says.

"I don't want you to leave," Annika says.

"Me neither. Trapped in a car with him and my parents? It'll feel like forever. But then I'll be away at school, and my life can start."

"You'll be free," Annika says. She hears the front door to the building creak open behind Summer.

Summer, suddenly ferocious, flies at Annika. "You're obsessed with me! Quit stalking me. The next time my boyfriend catches you lurking around here, he'll kill you! Do you understand me?" She looks worried for a second. Annika almost misses it. "I'm serious!" Summer shoves her so hard, Annika feels the bruises already forming on her chest. She imagines they're blue, like Summer's earrings. "Get out of here!"

Annika's eyes are round and wide. She does what she'd do if any vibrant bird flew into a tizzy and turned on her when all she's doing is admiring their beauty—the outside kind and the inside kind. She starts crying and blurts out "I'm so sorry" before taking off to run as fast as her shoes will permit.

When she is far enough away, she turns while still running to be sure no one is following her. She is not coordinated enough for all this multitasking. Her sneaker catches on the upraised edge of a pothole and sends her crashing to the pavement. She's relieved to realize she's no longer crying.

Annika knows Summer has needed her, too, in a way. If a bird flies and chirps above with no one to watch or hear, is there any point in soaring and singing up there at all? At least Summer's migration patterns are nothing if not predictable. She'll be back for a short spell in the cold winter with the tree outside her window as lonely and empty as Annika. She'll be back in the humid summer days, lazing around in those baggy tank tops she looks so fetching in. Annika has always planned on waiting. But she's wanted Summer to be free of the boyfriend, her parents, the tiny bedroom. Until now, it's never occurred to her that Summer might need to be free of Annika, too.

She stands up, humming her and Summer's shared favorite song to herself. She stares at the ground, and as the sun sets on her shoulders, she starts walking in the direction of home.

And There I'll Be

There is a fork in the road where they said they would meet again one day. This must be considered with a hefty sprinkling of indulgence. They were only ten years old at the time.

"You walk twenty steps past the Daltons' sky blue mailbox at the end of their drive. You can crane your neck much as you want, but you won't be able to see their house from there, so you probably shouldn't bother. It might as well be in another town, their driveway's so long. Mom says they need their own zip code behind those fancy pants gates of theirs," Cheyenne told Noah, veering off on a tangent from which they both knew she'd return shortly, when she felt like it. "She says next thing they'll be hiring some armed guards to man the place. Keep riff raff like us out."

Cheyenne hadn't paused to take a breath yet as she continued to draw a childish map into the red earth at his feet with a combination of her fingers and a nearby twig. Noah sat silent and attentive, as he always did while she talked with the breathless allure of someone who had quite a lot of important things to say. It wasn't one of those common situations, though, where she wished he'd talk more or he wished she'd talk less. He hoped she'd go on talking forever, and she hoped he'd go on listening forever, but those harmonious desires were put on temporary hold by her parents deciding to move just prior to the start of fifth grade.

Cheyenne would have been perfectly content to grow old in Stockton, New Jersey with her quiet companion. Together they would traverse dirt paths barefoot and cannonball into greenish brown canal water just beyond a crop of slick stones for as long as they were physically able, but her ambitious father had other plans. He couldn't become a household name Broadway sensation from the living room of a hundred-year-old stone farmhouse in South Jersey. A historic home he didn't even choose, but rather one that had been dropped in his lap by his wife's deceased parents who didn't believe in his dream.

Cheyenne was pretty sure she supported her father's hopes of stardom, but she was also afraid to leave the only home she'd ever known and Noah. Her father's pursuit of happiness had a way of directly interfering with hers and her mother's on just a regular Tuesday, but never more than now when he was uprooting them to a place neither of them wanted to be. The city that never closes its smoky eyes, just across the George Washington Bridge. Fine to visit, but Cheyenne's mother had instilled in her, since birth, the conviction that pretty girls like her got snatched up in a lawless land like that the minute they ventured outside, never to be seen again.

"Your odds of it happening are only increased if you spend too much time there," her mother reasoned. Her logic was sound, so Cheyenne had to agree. There would be no prancing barefoot on gravel roads littered with last night's condoms and used needles. That was certain.

It won't be so bad, Noah had murmured after she told him. She then pushed him up against their old oak tree, the one they'd talked about carving their names into but had never gotten around to it, and planted a kiss on his cool, chapped lips. It was the first for them both. She had always imagined doing so would taste like cinnamon, but it was more garlicky than she was expecting. We'll visit each other, he had continued, or maybe only his eyes had said that part. She couldn't remember words, only his way of looking at her.

"Anyway," Cheyenne said, on that last summer afternoon together, placing her warm hand on Noah's bare leg. "Once the trees start to be so tall and full that it gets hard to see the sun through them, you'll know you're there. And when you look up," she smiled, toothy and pleased with herself, "there I'll be."

**

It was only a high school graduation, quickie marriage, two kids, and a divorce later that set Cheyenne to reminiscing. She started to think that probably Noah was waiting for her at the fork. She had told him that's where she'd be when the time came. It certainly seemed to have arrived, she thought as she gazed into the rearview mirror. Her boys were arguing and shoving each other in the backseat of her '97 Honda. Her eyes held the tired distance of a mother whose adoration and resentment battle too often with a different winner each day.

Her parents scooped their grandchildren up in their arms when Cheyenne dropped them off without explanation that weekend, at their home in Connecticut. Her mother was covered in flour and smelled of cherries and almonds as she beckoned the rabble-rousing monsters into the kitchen. Her father, the voice over actor, followed and delighted them as he performed impressions of all their favorite TV characters.

Sometimes, Cheyenne felt bad for him that the whole stage thing hadn't panned out, but it was that silly failed fantasy of his that had wrenched her away from Noah to begin with. Besides, he often got stopped while he was out and about when passersby heard his booming voice and recognized it. They complimented him for the velvety smooth confidence his words drizzled over consumers as they watched various commercials and straight to video movie trailers. "I can't tell you how many cleaning products are sitting on my shelf that I don't even need, thanks to you," they'd chastise him with a twinkle in their tone. So the fame he'd sought when he fled Stockton was his in that diluted way.

**

Cheyenne started to wonder, as she entered New Jersey, if she should have forced herself to drink more water before setting out on this extended drive. Surely, dehydration was to blame for the mirage up ahead on the shoulder of the road. The teenage hitchhiker was Cheyenne's mirror image from a time before pregnancy and childbirth had done irreparable things to her. Demolished her figure, her energy, her ability to remember herself as anything more than Henry and Oscar's mom. Cheyenne blinked, turned down the radio, and slowed the car alongside the girl. She reached across the seat to crank the passenger side window down. "Hey," she called out. "You look like you need a ride."

The girl's profile was stony. "No. You can keep driving. Thanks."

Cheyenne smiled. "Don't be ridiculous. If you're not hitchhiking, what are you doing walking on the side of the road then?"

"What do you care? Maybe I'm just holding out for a nicer car." The girl turned and revealed her face, adorned with a mixture of contempt and fear.

Cheyenne began to feel silly. Her own color was wheat kissed with gold and the girl's was peaches dipped in milk. Her features were also striking and drawn in harsher lines than the ones on Cheyenne's soft, round face. Cheyenne's chin grew less defined with each passing year. Why exactly was she bothering this young stranger again? She really needed to drink some water.

"Sorry. Stay safe out here, okay?" Cheyenne prepared to speed up again as the honking of the cars behind her reached a frightening decibel.

The girl grunted. "Thanks. Had a fight with my boyfriend and got out. He'll go let off some steam and is gonna catch back up with me soon."

As Cheyenne drove off, she glanced into her rearview mirror. She blinked to unblur her temporarily cloudy vision. Nothing. It was like the girl had never been there at all.

**

Before long, as if by magic, Cheyenne found herself standing in front of the old white stucco house where Noah had lived. It was just a few feet from the foam green Stockton bridge. She could toss rocks into the water after this. Maybe she should do that first. So she did for a while. The Delaware stared at her, a little accusatory, as if wondering what she was doing here without Noah. He'd always been a much better shot than her anyway.

The house looked different than she remembered it, but this was it alright. There was a swing and a rocking chair on the front porch that hadn't been there before. Noah's parents used to just drag out chairs from the kitchen when they felt like sitting there. The wooden planks creaked beneath Cheyenne's feet like always, though. It was comforting. Like a forgotten, familiar song.

The woman who answered the door was very kind. Said she and her husband, newlyweds, hadn't owned it long. The previous occupants had been a much older couple with several dogs but no children. "So maybe your friend and his family were here even before them. I'm sorry. How long has it been?"

Cheyenne told her not to worry about it, thanked her, and went on her way.

After a brief stop at the old stone farmhouse her father had escaped, Cheyenne meandered a bit around town. She enjoyed herself at all of her and Noah's old haunts. Even went for a quick walk on the towpath, dipped her toes in the canal, and chatted with some men who were there fishing. She thought about how nice it would be to bring her sons here and share all this quiet beauty with them.

Soon, though, her desire to dawdle passed, and she knew there was only one place left to go. Once there, she made herself comfortable, settling in for the long haul. She sniffed the air for hints of cinnamon or garlic, but it just smelled fresh like spring after the rain.

**

Cheyenne shivered as the air grew colder and nibbled at her exposed skin. The setting sun's remaining warmth couldn't be felt here underneath the kingdom of trees clumped together that she had drawn for Noah so many years earlier. She wondered if the map meant to lead him to her was still there, stamped into the ground in her sloppy scrawl for all eternity.

Cheyenne heard a gentle crunch, like footsteps on dry leaves. Her eyes swiveled in the sound's general direction, but she only found a squirrel there, watching her. She imagined it asking her, really? You're still here?

"Yes," she said aloud, a bit sassy. "I am."

But no one tells you this is how it will be. That true love, the kind where being happy is actually an option, is really just waiting for something. And if that's all Noah is, something to wait for and believe in, then it's the only kind of love Cheyenne would ever want to know.

Cheyenne wasn't sure if she fell asleep waiting or if time had just escaped her, but when she opened her eyes, the darkness sent chills fluttering down her spine, like a spider soaring down an ethereal thread of its own weaving. As she hurried to stand up, she heard him say, You're really here. Or at least she thought she did. It was only ever that look dancing in Noah's eyes that lingered in her memory, not anything he said. She didn't ask now if it was him. Just melted forward into the arms she felt sure were there.

In Twenty Years

Being a nanny was not going to be Manju Gupta's full-time job forever. Her husband, Krishna, had only just graduated from law school and taken the bar exam. They were waiting for his new job as tax attorney at the firm of Bundy, Willis, and Brown to begin in the fall. She had not so recently earned her degree in philosophy and still didn't know what she wanted to be when she grew up. The newlyweds repeatedly had an argument that went something like this:

"The wedding was expensive. It's time to start saving money, Manju. We have student loans and bills to pay. You can't just be a stay-at-home wife yet. We can't afford it."

"I don't want to stay home permanently, just until I figure things out. Why can't you understand that?"

"It's not just you anymore," he said. "There are two of us to think about now. And maybe a family someday."

Finally, one day, Krishna won the battle. Manju had to get a job.

The new job at the Thompson family's home had Manju more than a little nervous. The last diaper she'd changed had been her brother, Naveen's, nine years earlier. She had treasured Naveen when he was small, as if he were her own little doll. She had liked to rock and cradle him and play mother.

Manju's parents had been supportive when she approached them about her fears, after the crutch of her student identity was gone. The only thing in this life she was certain of anymore was the strength and endurance of Krishna's love and devotion. All else concerning who she was supposed to become was a gray haze. Her parents reminded her of how warm and natural she'd been with her brother and suggested the temporary financial fix of being a nanny. This surprised Manju since her only babysitters growing up had been her grandparents and her parents' fellow Indian immigrant friends. No outsiders had ever been considered for the position. She was unsure of what it would be like to work in a stranger's home.

Standing at the Thompson's front door, about to ring the bell, she contemplated an escape. There was no time to run, however, as she met the large dark eyes of a woman peering out at her through the glass to the right of the door. A tattoo of black and purple flowers sprouted along the woman's brown neck like vines of ivy and clung there like weeds. Her hair was wild and free, but her irises, already delving their way into Manju's flesh with bruising fingertips, were caged.

**

"Don't go yet. I can't bear to be alone with the baby." Sona's hand fluttered up to her forehead in a dramatic imitation of swooning. "I don't survive long after you leave me each day." She smiled in the charming manner of a child confident in their ability to get what they want.

"Sona, please don't start. I'm tired," Manju said, trying to suppress a groan at her employer's customary and effective wheedling. "You'll be fine. He's not carrying any concealed weapons. You're safe until Jon gets home." Manju's position was strict defense in this daily game they played.

"I know you judge me." Sona sighed. "Why wouldn't you? Afraid of my own baby."

"Sona—"

"You'll stay then? Chai's almost ready."

Manju nodded. Of course she lost this round. Sona was the type who always won. Besides, keeping her company meant less time for Manju to be alone at home waiting for Krishna. He worked unthinkably long hours that first year.

Sona was an older mother. She had gotten pregnant at thirty-nine, and now, at forty, she and her husband, Jon, were new parents to a beautiful baby boy. Sona and her family had left India when she was twelve and moved to New York City; it was there she met Jon Thompson at the youthful age of twenty. They traveled the world together like nomads, eventually settling in New Jersey.

Sona owned and ran her business on the internet, selling sustainable clothes that she'd designed and made by hand herself. Saris, salwar kameez, kurtis, peasant blouses, skirts, and pants in a range of fabrics and brilliant colors. Manju liked to run her fingers along them before leaving—some soft and deep like she was dunking her hands in a jug full of milk, while others were sturdy, stiff, and scratched back.

Sona was in the house all day with Manju and the baby, but was always shut up in her office until about four o'clock in the afternoon. Then while the baby napped, she would come join Manju in the kitchen and guilt her out of fleeing right away. They would chat before Manju left, the time they spent together growing longer each day as the months passed. Some days they laughed. A few times, Manju even spoke about herself. But mostly, Manju just listened.

Sitting together at the old and worn kitchen table now, over steaming hot mugs of masala chai, Manju wondered why she bothered pretending to put up a fight when they both knew she'd linger anyway. Perhaps because it was such a dependable part of their routine. Sona chattered as the minutes swelled into an hour or more.

After there was no more tea and Sona had run out of stories to tempt her with, Manju stood up. "All right. I'm really going now."

Sona laughed. "Okay. That's fair. He'll be back soon anyway." Her face darkened. "If you lived here, I wouldn't mind if he never came home." Sona lowered her volume. "He's so—"

They both heard the front door creak open and made an abrupt switch to Tamil, as they often did, with Manju helping to remind Sona of the many words and expressions she'd forgotten from her mother tongue. Sona said she liked to speak Tamil with Manju because Jon didn't know any.

When Jon entered the kitchen, he frowned and asked what Manju was still doing there.

**

One afternoon, Jon came home earlier than usual. He greeted Manju, and they made polite small talk before he left the room and joined Sona upstairs in her office. They were talking a while until Manju even forgot they were both home. Then Sona's voice boomed throughout the house.

"There you go with the same old excuses. Has the baby made me that disgusting?"

"Sona, don't be ridiculous. We're both exhausted. I don't see you ever in the mood either. But go ahead. Just blame me."

"This wouldn't even be an issue if we'd never had the baby, so you are to blame for that."

Manju was getting herself a glass of water and had the baby, asleep in his bassinet, in the kitchen with her. At these last words of Sona's, Manju frowned and glided over to the baby to make sure the noise hadn't woken him. Satisfied that he remained asleep, she lowered herself to the floor beside him. She pushed and pulled the bassinet back and forth in a slow, peaceful rhythm. She was used to Sona and Jon's screaming matches now, and the little attention they paid to the fact that she was there in the house hearing every word, but they never failed to upset her and excite her compassion for the little boy in her charge.

Sona walked in and just barely glanced at Manju, not acknowledging the scene from upstairs. She delicately eased her small baby boy out of the bassinet, nestling him in her arms. She went and sat down at the table, slinging him awkwardly over her shoulder. She began to talk as though she and Manju had been in the middle of a conversation. "That ass thinks he's entitled to a happy marriage because he gave me a ring and walked down an aisle twenty years ago. It takes work. Jon used to look at me like I was the most beautiful woman he'd ever seen. That was a long time ago. They look at you differently when you're young. Everyone treats you differently when you're young."

Manju nodded as if she knew anything about it but kept her mouth shut. The baby began to cry. Low pitched at first but quickly rising into a loud wail. Sona rubbed his back and bounced him roughly, kissing him all over, trying to make him stop. His crying only got louder and louder until Manju couldn't hear herself think. Sona pressed him to her brown breasts, which were peeking out over the habitually low-cut blouse she wore. She bent over him, her black frizzy hair tickling his cheeks, while she crooned a soft lullaby into his ear that Manju's own mother had sung to her and Naveen many a night, too. The baby wouldn't stop screaming. Sona then made an irritated sound from deep within her throat and rammed her chair back as she thrust the baby at Manju.

"Take him!"

Sona stormed into the living room and slammed around in there for a few minutes while Manju held the baby and rocked him back and forth without a sound. He kept crying, but the volume was decreasing. She kept her pace steady. Within a few minutes, his cries ceased and he was asleep again.

Sona peeked into the room. She pantomimed clapping. "You're a miracle," she whispered, returning to her seat. She wiped her forehead, staring at her son. "God, I hate being a mother."

Manju tensed and walked the baby back over to his bassinet and placed him there without looking back at Sona as she spoke. "You don't mean that."

"I do. I really do. You don't know." Sona was passionate in her tone.

"Fine. I just wish you wouldn't say things like that to me. I have to go. I'll see you tomorrow." Manju grabbed her purse and headed straight for the door without a backwards glance. She made it outside before she was stopped by the pity in Sona's voice behind her.

"I was you once, you know. Twenty years ago. I was you."

Manju turned around, halfway down the brick path leading to the sidewalk. Sona stood in the doorway, her head tilted to the side as she observed Manju.

"What?"

"I was the same way, all pretty and sweet. Excited for what life and my future with Jon had in store for me. I was you."

Manju nodded but didn't respond. She turned away and continued the walk to her car.

**

Nearly two months later, Sona sat down across from Manju, sliding over a cup of chai. After a few quiet sips of her own drink, she said, apropos of nothing, "I'm not the monster you think I am. Jon and I agreed on no children, you know."

Manju couldn't conceal the surprise and interest that flickered across her features. "How'd you end up with one then?"

"Jon told me he'd gone to get the vasectomy. He was lying. We were totally unprotected and then I was throwing up all the time and, well, you know the rest."

Manju opened her mouth to speak. To say how she couldn't even comprehend a betrayal that deep. To say how sorry she was that Sona couldn't trust Jon anymore. To say it still wasn't the baby's fault, and now he's here, and Sona should try harder to love him. But in keeping with what made her so likable and necessary to Sona, she kept her lips closed and her thoughts to herself.

"Sometimes I feel closer to you than my husband," Sona said. "Sometimes I think I love you more than him."

Manju tried to glare at her, but instead she just stared too long, more intense and pointed than she intended. "You shouldn't say things like that when you're angry. You don't mean them. You two just fought this morning."

"You make me feel so much better all the time. I really love having you here. Our talks, most of the time, they're the happiest and very best part of my week." Sona stared back, her bright eyes demanding a response.

Manju was looking down at the table now, deep in thought. She traced the imperfections and ragged cracks in the aged brown wood with her fingertip of the same shade. She was absorbing everything Sona said, even if she didn't feel up to resuming eye contact.

"I just meant you understand me better than he does. You listen to me so well. Jon's a damn brick wall. He doesn't listen to me like you do. No one does."

"A therapist would," Manju said, more to herself than anyone.

"What?"

"Nothing. I think you should see someone, Sona. Get some help for how you're feeling. It doesn't have to be so hard every day. Things can get better."

"You're right." Sona reached across the table. Manju didn't notice, her eyes still fixed on a spot on its hard surface. Sona placed a rough palm on Manju's cheek, gliding it across her smooth skin, much like Manju's hands did daily over the garments upstairs. Manju started, but didn't move away either. She was now looking directly at her companion, a blush creeping into her face. Sona moved her hand to brush stray dark tendrils back from Manju's forehead.

"You're so beautiful and fresh and pure, Manju. You make me believe things can get better."

Manju jumped up, nearly falling in her haste. She backed away a few steps, groping for her jacket hanging on the back of the chair. Sona stood up, looking genuinely confused, and began to approach her, her expression open and pleading.

"Don't," Manju said.

Sona stopped where she was and put her hands up as if to prove her harmlessness. They both waited, completely still. Then Sona took one more step forward. "I think you've misunderstood me."

"I'll leave. I am leaving." Manju turned to go, her skin so hot it was burning.

"Wait."

Manju pivoted slightly. The tired look Sona usually wore was back on her face.

"I'm sorry I made you uncomfortable." Sona paused, appearing thoughtful and lost in equal measure. "I was just trying to tell you—well, it doesn't matter, does it? I'm wrong to try and put everything on your shoulders. It's really not your problem. Go on home, and I'll see you Monday."

**

After a weekend of being unable to stop wondering about Sona in ways she didn't quite want to understand, Manju stood at the Thompsons' front door. The words "I quit" hesitated at the threshold of her lips. Before she could reach for the bell, Jon wrenched the door open.

"Sona?" He stared past Manju, his voice frantic, the baby wailing in his arms. The child was now big enough to start crawling soon. "Sona, where are you?" Jon said to no one in particular, his eyes darting around and finally zeroing in on Manju. "I'm sure you know. Is she really gone?"

Manju began to sputter, guilt welling up in her chest as though he was right to suspect her of being complicit in whatever the hell Sona had done now. "I'm so sorry—I really don't know what's going on."

"Tell me the truth." His tone was pained but his expression ferocious. "She told you everything like you were her goddamn diary. So don't pretend you didn't know she was leaving." Manju tried to cut in, but he raised his volume as he leaned in closer. "Was it someone else? An affair?" He grabbed at Manju's wrist, but she yanked it out of his reach. Breathless, he whispered, "Was it you?"

Manju looked at the baby, thankful his eyes were closed as he cried, so she could force herself not to feel as she said, "I can't work here anymore."

"Good," Jon said, retreating into the house. "Daycare will be better for him than you or his mother." The door closed, and Manju was suddenly aware of how loudly she could hear herself breathing.

When Manju reached home, she went straight to her laptop to email Sona and demand an explanation. Jon hadn't gotten around to specifying what she'd taken with her, so Manju was too afraid of trying Sona's cell and having him answer. She checked if there was already a message in her inbox waiting for her. Nothing. Furious, she refreshed the page. Still nothing. Refresh. No new messages.

Manju slumped back in her chair, disbelief and hurt coursing through every nerve in her body. A pressure built in her chest. She ached for some final words. But perhaps this is what Sona had been trying to tell her only a few days earlier, trying to prepare her, but Manju had been too afraid to listen. Too afraid to wait and stay for the word—goodbye—she didn't know she dreaded but now knew she needed.

The screen blurred and the words on it began to swim. Manju wiped her eyes dry with violent hands. A sound in the room jolted her. She swiveled around in her chair and saw Krishna standing there.

"I forgot some papers here, but I have to be quick getting back—" He stopped when he saw the look on her face.

He rushed over to her, his arms outstretched. She reached for him, and he drew her into a tight hug. She gripped his muscular arms, the arms that held her so close each night, keeping her safe and warm. She pulled back to look at him.

The truth was plain, that neither of them could really know what this or any other life would be for them years from now. And yet Manju stared into his eyes, seeing the earnestness there, and wanted so badly to believe.

The Suitor

Straightening the place settings and adjusting chairs is not enough to occupy her distracted mind. She glances out the window, not expecting to see anything different from when she'd last looked a moment earlier but unable to avoid the impulse. No figure coming up the walk yet—just an inky sky with jagged, harsh clouds scattered across it. The mood is not calculated to stir romantic sentiments in her breast or her visitor's. She couldn't control the weather when she extended the invitation, and now they will have to make do. She wonders if the distant rumbles of thunder will prevent him from traveling to her small home on the rocky waterfront.

The night is warm in spite of the imminent threat of a storm. The lightning flashes cannot be seen from her kitchen, and the thunder following the strikes takes so long to sound and is so much more like a murmur than a clap that she doubts it will approach any time soon. The waves lapping up on the sand do not look dangerous but rather gloomy. If he cancels now at the last minute when the rain hasn't even begun and they've had this plan for weeks, she will be sure to forget him and put this whole stressful business behind her.

Reaching into the dark cherrywood cabinet for a wine glass, she pauses to caress the stem. The glasses she and her late husband clinked on their wedding day. Perhaps it would be too much to serve wine to the suitor in these. She returns it to its place, her hand shaking from a slight tremble. Thinking of her late husband when she is already so nervous is a terrible idea. It is less about if he would mind her taking up with another man. What bothers her more is if he himself would have liked the suitor enough to spend an evening with him.

The picture she selected to represent herself on the internet had been honest and modest. Her son, photography being the latest of his hobbies, captured it with his new tripod on a visit without his wife and children. He positioned her to face the sunshine yellow front door with the vast ocean behind her on a drizzly, misty day. Her hair was thinning, gray, and whipping around her face. The lenses of her red square rimmed glasses were peppered and flecked with the spray of water droplets. The gold in her brown eyes twinkled. When her son e-mailed her the photo, she smiled at her own face. It was the first time she felt vain in a very long time. This was the image that prompted the suitor to "wink" at her on the dating site she'd so hesitantly joined.

The suitor has a bit of a roguish charm to him. Still harmless. Old fashioned. But each time his jokes are sly, or a compliment turns her cheeks the color of bitten plum's flesh, she finds herself questioning him, her, and the whole thing again.

Now he is late. Only by a few minutes, yes, but her husband was never late. Not once. Not ever in forty years. The suitor has only been in existence to her for a few months, and on this, their first meeting, he's late.

She can't be picky anymore. Not now that her husband is dead, her son is busy, his wife is frigid and distant, and his daughters are fast entering their preteen years with less interest to spare for their grandmother. No matter how long the suitor makes her wait, she finds that the mere dream of him has become necessary to help her escape this gnawing ache.

When she read the email in which the suitor first suggested they meet, she slammed her laptop shut. Her heart thudded as she walked outside, hugging her shawl close, protecting her from the wind and what felt like her late husband's judgment descending upon her. She didn't know this man at all.

So they both typed a few words on their computers and saw one picture of each other. He didn't know that nothing made her feel more alive than wading out into the unruly ocean on a gray day and breathing in the salty air. He didn't know that she used to teach high school English before her son made being a mother her full time job. Or that there had been a several year drought in her marriage during which she fantasized about the feel of another man's skin against hers daily. It didn't matter who—just any other man besides the one in her bed, the one she loved whose ring shackled her antsy finger.

Yet now, here she is. Her elbows propped up on the counter. Jiggling her right foot like an awkward teenager. Her eyelashes feel uncomfortably thick and twined. She glances out the window once more. The black silhouette of a man gleams against the darkening sky. His shape grows larger as it draws closer. She turns away. A clap of thunder coincides with the sound of knuckles rapping on the bright yellow door as the wind whispers through the room, kissing her on the cheek.

Rose Petals and Obligations

Every year on the day Mina's victim perished, Luke would drive to the boy's house and wait outside in his car until both parents had left for work. Then he would go and slip an envelope of money under their front door.

Sometimes he wondered what the boy would have grown up to be. Who he would have become if Mina hadn't snuffed out his flame before he'd had a chance for it to catch fire and really dance. It had only flickered before Mina whispered and extinguished it, like the small waxy candles on her birthday cakes each year.

At times, Luke's wonderings got confused. His imagination wandered down paths that didn't exist, twisting and bending reality, until the boy was his and Mina's son that they'd lost. And then he grieved even harder than he'd ever grieved for him when he was just a helpless stranger who crossed their path by unforgiving coincidence. It became easier to forget this way that he and Mina had never actually had any children of their own or even gotten married, leaving them with no tangible links to tie them together after they parted ways. Only the invisible bonds of memories and disappointments.

"We don't deserve to have any children," she said when their efforts at getting pregnant failed yet again. "Not after what we did."

Then they thought of the boy's parents together, in agonizing silence so thick they couldn't find each other through it. His hurt made no dent in her resolve. She just stared out the window, though with the curtains closed, she couldn't see outside.

Luke had held Mina close, eight years earlier, as they danced cheek to cheek on cobblestones under the streetlights on Montmartre. With him humming *la vie en rose* into her ear.

"You can hardly claim to be drunk on only one glass of wine," he said as she swayed away from him afterward, her movements unsteady and hypnotic. He said the same thing three years later as they left their favorite restaurant, arguing over who was sober enough to drive.

The sky was a rigid obsidian, and the street winding through the woods that Mina preferred to the busy highway was quiet with no lights anywhere. When their car thudded, rough and violent, they both breathed, "deer", before continuing home, shaken.

It wasn't until they saw the boy on the news in daylight—he'd been getting high with his friends in the woods and ambled over to the road to get better service on his cell—that the fear of possibilities gripped them and wouldn't let go.

The boy glided through each room of their small yellow and white house, caressing their skin with shivers on the off chance they'd forgotten him. He speckled Luke's strawberry blonde hair with silver. He drew lines and pressed creases into Mina's face, one for each year he'd been dead. The boy watched as the silence between Luke and Mina billowed and rippled like strong trees with weak branches in merciless winds, littering the ground with leaves too tired and dry to fight anymore.

The day finally came when Mina said she was going to turn herself in. "Just sleep on it," Luke pleaded with her. So she did. And in the morning, they didn't go to the police station together. He went through his usual getting ready routine and drove to work. She, on the other hand, packed her clothes and books into a suitcase and left forever.

Haunted as they'd been, the world had still managed to drizzle rose petals every so often—thick as satin, airy as silk. Luke never sang to Mina again, but the tune lingered in their heads anyway. But after she left him and the obligation to protect her and her guilt had long since atrophied, the sky was flowerless.

One morning, as Luke sat in his Chevy outside the boy's home, quite unsure if his parents still even lived there or if he'd been financing another set of strangers all these years, he thought he saw Mina's head of wild curls across the street, her brown eyes staring straight ahead. He didn't go check to be certain. He preferred to imagine her there, sitting in a car like his, nursing a debt that could never be repaid.

Ships in the Night

1.

Lalita breathed in the cold air as it swirled around her and licked her cheeks raw with a stinging finality. As it entered her chest and lungs, it seemed to freeze her from the inside and snake its way into the pockets of uncertainty she still felt about her decision, filling them up with cracked ice that stabbed at those spots most vulnerable. She opened her mouth and watched white mist spool out of it in puffs.

She was seated atop the banks of the Delaware River, on the Pennsylvania side, usually a vast green and brown landscape littered with sticks and branches hurled there by sporadic storms and violent winds. Now, though, it was a sea of blinding white, the ground concealed by thick sheets of hard snow. Seemingly soft and powdery from a distance but, in reality, harsh and rough to the touch like stone.

She was leaving him today, though he didn't know it. She planned to make a clean break of it. It wasn't one specific word or action that had precipitated the plan. It had all been building below the surface for so long that, like an iceberg, it threatened complete destruction and devastation if they didn't change course soon.

2.

"So you're leaving her just like that?" Donna couldn't keep the morbid fascination out of her voice.

"Better that it be fast. Don't want to drag it out and hurt her anymore than necessary. And besides, it's not just like that. It's been a long time coming." Sanjay fidgeted with his necktie and readjusted the position of his silverware to be parallel with his plate.

"You could try a separation?" Donna saw a wrinkle in his jacket sleeve and reached out to smooth it for him. Her hand then remained there. His eyes snapped up to meet hers, but he didn't move his arm away.

"She used to steam them."

"What?"

"My suits, I mean. Iron, press, steam—whatever they needed, she was always on top of it. I never had to think about if they were ready to wear to court or not. They just were."

Donna's eyes glittered playfully. "Surely that's not why you're abandoning ship now?"

He forced a smile that looked more like a grimace. "Of course not. Don't be stupid. Anyway, a separation? No, definitely not. Just dangles the false promise of a reconciliation. No. Where is our check?"

3.

Lalita could only think of him with irritation now. Just that morning, he'd helped to fortify her resolve.

"Toast?" he'd asked.

"No thanks."

"You've hardly eaten for days. You'll be hungry. Let me just fix you some toast."

"I said I'm fine."

Always thinking he knew best. He didn't know what was best for her.

If he did, maybe she'd be hugging the twins right now instead of her own knees to her chest.

4.

"I'm so sorry. I never knew that happened." Donna leaned forward to take hold of and caress Sanjay's trembling hand.

"How could you? It was all before you joined the firm, and it's not something I talk about." Sanjay eased his hand out of hers. "I try to never even think about it."

"Losing them both—it didn't bring you and your wife closer together?"

"At first it did, while it was all happening in the hospital. We were each other's life preservers. If we didn't hold on, we couldn't have stayed afloat."

"So what changed?"

"She did. Once it became real, that they were gone and not coming back, she started to blame me." Sanjay closed his eyes and massaged his temples. "The doctor told me while she was unconscious and hooked up to all those machines—she'll never understand what that was like. I really thought I was going to lose her. He said it was her or the babies. That if they didn't come out right away, she wouldn't survive. But that if he took them out so early, they probably wouldn't."

"Oh, Sanjay." Donna's voice now hushed, she sat back in her chair.

"Doesn't she know it haunts me every day? That it killed me? I did what I had to do. She slept. I was awake. I had no choice. I didn't know that if I kept her alive, our marriage would die along with them."

5.

In Lalita's imagination, the twins had grown up to enjoy lazily tubing down the river with her, one of her favorite pastimes in the sweltering summers. At night, in her mind, they created many a memory floating and laughing together.

As she stared out onto the choppy steel colored Delaware now, her eyes devoid of feeling and awareness, it morphed into a golden blue instead, both warm and inviting. "Amma! C'mon, faster!" her children would urge her, she was sure of it. "You're practically asleep."

She'd shake her head at them, lazily drifting along, allowing the river to carry her as it may, respecting its slow and easy pace. "This isn't a race. It's a beautiful day and they don't last. Just enjoy it." Lalita would tilt her head back further, dipping the frizzy ends of her hair into the green tinged water and basking in the friendly glow of the sunlight sprinkled across her face like raindrops.

Somehow she knew they wouldn't have been like her. They'd have been like Sanjay, plagued by his eternal impatience with whatever activity lay before him, always longing for and imagining what could be next. What could be better.

6.

"Come on," Donna said. "Let's head back to work." Her expression made clear that Sanjay was to come pull her chair out for her. He sat there for almost an uncomfortable passage of time before getting up to do so.

"Sure. I just need to make a quick stop at home first." Sanjay rested a casual hand on the small of her back as they departed the diner.

7.

The wind continued to howl and whip Lalita's dark hair around her face at an ever increasing rate. As darkness began to settle in on her and the bare trees, she felt closer to the meaning of it all than ever before. Some almost lyrical voice of wisdom seemed to speak to her and fill the cold, empty silence that was threatening to swallow her whole.

She stood and took one more deep breath of the inexorable winter air. She slowly began to weave her way down the snowy bank, sidestepping the slippery patches, until she could feel the water caressing her feet. The shouting of the panicked voice behind her was muffled and unimportant as she descended further into the cold, treacherous water, spreading her arms out and pushing away the jagged shards of ice surrounding her with numb fingertips.

Probably Sanjay found the note. He must have gone home early. She'd better hurry.

As she lowered her head beneath the dark gray water and the cold stole through her veins, she felt her muscles seize up. And yet the painful tight tension in her chest lifted for the first time in years. She thought she saw their smiling faces as she prepared to finally join them.

How Then

1.

It was little Parvati who first tested out the "walk a mile in another man's shoes" theory. She learned it could be done at dusk in the shadowy lot bridging her small town's drug store and yoga studio.

2.

She'd been imagining her older sister, Pooja—her fair and lovely skin, her liquid orb irises that cast moonlight on all in their path—when she remembered the perky platitude.

So she crammed her wide feet into her sister's spotless Keds at just the time, in just the place.

Her bones and limbs lengthened until they almost splintered. Her ribs ached as the chest perched above them grew heavy and full. Her lips swelled as her belly curved inward. Her cheeks hollowed and bloomed pink. Her eyes shimmered.

3.

Little Parvati had never been the object of so much attention before. Never shrunk under the gaze of so many hungry, intimidating, demanding creatures. Never heard so many words reduce her to nothing more than a pair of breasts and legs.

She remembered the night her sister came home from a date with her eyes wet and her skirt torn. At the time, Parvati thought Pooja was silly and vain to cry over such a mild injury to her precious clothes.

The breath of the monsters hot on her skin, Parvati shivered in her sister's shoes until her borrowed bones rattled. She wrenched herself free of their insistent fingers, certain of what she must do.

4.

Parvati stared at her reflection in the store window, cringing and wincing, as she scarred her temporary face with a rock.

She had to see to it that her sister's beauty could never hurt her again. They would be plain and safe together.

Nurture

When Esme joined her father in his garden, they rarely exchanged words of much consequence. Usually, no matter what she asked him, regardless of how specific the topic, Aakash Acharya responded with a bare bones comment on the elements. He would praise or bemoan their effects on his neat, tightly controlled square of nature in their otherwise shaggy backyard. They saved uncomfortable details for inside the house. Out here, she knew, was his sanctuary away from his daughter's problems. Here, only these more easily governed fruits of his labor existed.

"Dad, I need to talk to you about something." Esme was irritated but unsurprised when he didn't answer. At least his distraction meant a delay in the penetrating, severe stare she was sure to receive. She felt silly for still allowing his quiet judgment to rile her up and his placid evasion of real, honest conversation to hurt her, after enduring three long decades of both. Upon each return to her childhood home in Bensalem, Pennsylvania, time sped backward until she was small again, and then it stood still there.

Today, they surveyed his begonias together in tense silence. Today, Esme would have to tell him about losing her temp job at the mayor's office and the impending eviction from her studio apartment in Philadelphia— the one he was still guarantor for on the lease. Today, she would have to ask him for his help. But first, his plants.

"Stem rot," her father said finally, shaking his head at the wilting flowers. "I've been watering them extra to make up for this drought but— well, look at them, Esme." The tone of disappointment with which he muttered her name was, of course, directed at that aforementioned fickle twist of the earth's plans, but it made Esme bristle with discomfort anyway.

Esme had been Esme for as long as she could remember, but as her older sister liked to sternly remind her, she'd once been Easwari. That was the name on her birth certificate, and Ambika was the name on her sister's. Their mother, Amrita, had never been a proud Indian like Aakash. When they were young, she had taken a liking that almost bordered on obsession to old black and white French films. Easwari became Esme and never looked back. Ambika became Amelie, but at age seven, she demanded to know why they had such European names. Why their names contrasted so starkly with their brown skin. Her mother's answer—to help them fit in better—hadn't satisfied her, so she was reborn that day as Ambika.

"It's not too late to embrace your true identity," her sister had warned when Esme was fourteen. Her ominous words clashed with her dulcet tones as she prepared for the move to college in California that would leave Esme to handle their parents all on her own. "If you're not careful, you'll get all self-loathing like Amma, forever trying to please the wrong people."

Today, in Aakash's garden, surrounded by doomed begonias and dull Thai basil leaves, Esme tried to talk shop with her father while ducking for cover from the cool droplets of his advice before they picked up speed and ballooned into the kind of hail that can crack a windshield.

"We've got some rain in the forecast coming up," Esme said. "I'm sure that'll take care of things in no time."

Aakash didn't even glance up, but if he were the type to roll his eyes, she's sure he would right now. "That's not how gardens work, Esme." He finally turned to watch her as closely as he was capable in his emotionally limited fashion. "That's not how life works." Oh no. Ambika, that traitor, had already filled him in on at least some of it. "You can't just sit back and wait for everything to get better. Hoping it'll all just sort itself out. Or that some savior will come along to take care of it for you."

Esme felt her eyes narrow and a sneer begin to lift the corner of her upper lip, a defense mechanism developed in her early adolescence. His criticism couldn't injure her when she had a shield of scorn for his opinion to protect her. "I thought we were talking about your flowers, Dad." "You know exactly what we're talking about, Esme. You have to prepare for the storm before it gets here." She finished this last sentence aloud with him, a sign of disrespect she knew he hated. "Okay, okay. If you've just come here to be a smartass and you're too good for my help, you know how to get to the train station." He was already halfway to the back door before she caught up to him. She halted his progress with a light touch of her hand on his arm.

"I'm sorry, Dad. You're right. I don't plan ahead like I should." They waited in silence for what they both knew was coming next. "I'll need some money. And to stay here. But just for a little while." She heard herself talking faster, the panic rising in her throat. Was thirty the number? Was this the age when he'd finally say, *No, suck it up buttercup, you're on your own* and then really stick to it? Wasn't this the procrastinated point by when she was supposed to have magically transformed into an adult?

"Fine. Your mother's been visiting Mimi Auntie in Delaware for a few weeks, though, so it'll just be you and me here."

"Oh." This was unwelcome news. "Why didn't you go with her?"

Her father pulled a face. "Please. They'll have a much easier time gossiping about their husbands if we're not sitting there staring at them the whole time."

"True." Esme swallowed hard. "Anyway, thanks Dad, this really—"

"Don't get too comfortable. I don't want to be known as the pushover dad on the block with his fifty-year-old kid still living in the basement." He went inside, and she didn't follow.

**

"Pancakes?" Aakash was at the stove the next morning, surrounded by an array of sticky eggshells, flour, sugar, salt, and blueberries. He wasn't one for cooking, but it had always been a Saturday morning ritual at their house for Amrita to sleep in while Aakash and the girls made pancakes together. Esme couldn't help but feel a bit touched that he was making them today, on their first awkward morning of living together as adults. Maybe he was trying to make up for his harshness the day before. Esme took a seat at the island.

"Sure, thanks."

"I've been meaning to ask you." Aakash paused. "Are you still seeing that boy, Matthew?"

Only her father would refer to a grown man as a boy just because Esme liked him. "No. It's sort of fizzled out." She stretched and yawned, hoping that would be it on the subject.

"Well," Aakash said, "that's a relief at least. He was a waste of your time. But fizzling doesn't sound over." He cleared his throat. "Best to make a clean break when it comes to these things."

"Will do." After Matthew had cheated on her with a co-worker on a business trip, Esme broke up with him in theory. But they were still technically hooking up on and off, whenever loneliness and a longing for the comfort of past happiness overtook her. Each time she got dressed afterward, she mentally promised herself this would be the last one, but then he'd call or text, and there they'd go again.

Esme didn't feel up to sharing any of this with her father, now or ever. Ambika had already been unbearable enough, immediately offering to set Esme up with every Indian man they'd ever bumped into on the street.

"So when does Mom get back anyway?" Esme inhaled deeply, enjoying the scent of vanilla permeating the kitchen.

"Oh, I don't know," her father said, his back to her. "Soon, I'd imagine."

Esme frowned. "You don't know when she'll be back?"

Aakash's voice was gruff this time. "I just answered you, didn't I? It's not like she needs a date for a plane ticket. She drove." The brief silence that followed was broken only by the crackle of batter sizzling in the pan.

"She was supposed to come back a few days ago, but I don't know." He turned to face Esme. "She decided to stay a bit longer, I guess."

Esme got up and went to the cupboard for some plates so they wouldn't have to look at each other. She stopped in front of the window. "Oh, sorry, Dad. Looks like no rain today."

**

A week of sun dappled days slipped away uneventfully. Their annoyed discomfort with each other as roommates ebbed into more of a quiet understanding. Esme began to notice her father in the house a lot more. Less and less time was spent out in his beloved garden, and she couldn't fathom why. When the third week began and he still hadn't ventured out into the yard, she grew concerned but had no clue how to approach him about it.

"Dad?"

"What?" He was in his recliner—the same one he'd purchased when he and her mother had first come to America. He was watching some Hindi film without subtitles which was a not so subtle hint that Esme shouldn't bother joining him. He took a sip of whiskey neat without looking up at her in the doorway.

"What do you mean what? It's like 3 pm on a Tuesday." She motioned at the nearly empty glass in his hand. "What are you doing?"

"Isn't the point of being retired that you don't have to suffer responsibilities anymore? I don't have anywhere to be right now. Or tomorrow morning. So I'm having a drink with my movie." He lifted up the remote with his other hand and raised the volume. Normally, this would have been enough to make her leave.

"Dad, where's Mom?"

"This again." He pointed to the kitchen behind her. "Go get yourself a drink if you want. Otherwise, let me watch this in peace." When she remained where she was, he shifted in his seat. "Shouldn't you be looking for a job?"

"Your flowers are dying," Esme snapped before turning and walking out.

**

"Ambika? What the hell is going on? Where is Mom?" Esme was hiding in the empty bathtub that she and her sister had shared and fought over so many years earlier. She had the old, mildewy, beige curtains drawn to better conceal her, as if her father would ever burst in on her and enter a place so unappealing to him as the girls' old bathroom. Her slim phone felt hot and tingly pressed up against her ear. "Dad's claiming it's just some extended visit with Mimi Auntie that keeps getting longer, but he's obviously lying. I went into their room the other day. Her closet looks like it's been ransacked."

"Oh, I thought you knew," Ambika said. She was as infuriating as she was informed.

"Well, I don't."

"She's felt weird calling you because you're staying there right now. She figured he'd be the one to tell you."

"He didn't," Esme said, struggling to keep her voice even.

"No one's told you?"

Esme hated when her know-it-all sister belabored the obvious in that honeyed, innocent tone. "Seriously? Would I be calling to ask you if they did, genius?"

"Settle down," Ambika said, slightly more authoritative and forbidding now. Esme could imagine her rising up straighter and knitting her perfectly shaped eyebrows together on the other end. She could also picture Ambika in her immaculate Pacific Palisades mansion in California with her husband, Mohinder the entertainment lawyer, playing tennis with a client on their private court out back.

"Okay, sorry. Would you tell me? Quit stalling and just tell me."

"Fine. It's really her or him that you should be asking." Ambika hesitated, but this time, Esme did not rush her. "Amma says it's something of a trial separation. She just wants some time to think."

"Are you serious? And Dad knows? But hasn't told me?"

"He definitely knows," Ambika said. "He knew when she left. I think he assumed she'd get what she needed and come back by now."

"Well, has he said anything to you?"

"Yeah. He's pretty torn up about the whole thing. You know Amma, though. She can be selfish. Thinks she's the only one in the world with feelings." Ambika always put their mother down in that removed, academic tone, as if she were a counselor discussing a patient instead of a daughter her mother. Esme neglected to tell her sister how much it hurt that their father could confide in Ambika that he had any feelings at all.

That night, Esme tiptoed around Aakash. The last thing she wanted to do was bring up the truth she now knew. Somehow, it was like he'd figured her snooping out on his own anyway, because he was more distant and cold than ever.

"Do I need to set a deadline?" he asked after dinner, his voice as hard as ice. "For you to get a new job and find your own place? I'm not doing you any favors, the longer you hang around here, putting it off."

"No. I'm looking. There's not a lot of openings right now, but I am on it. Really."

He grunted in disbelief. Mom wasn't here to excuse her today, to plead with him that people are different. That the world is made up of individuals. That you can't hold everyone to the same impossibly high standards all the time. Especially not when they're down. *Esme isn't Ambika,* she'd tell him if she were here, deep affection and concern for her youngest lacing her voice and filling her light brown eyes. But Amrita, her beautiful mother, as stubborn and impetuous as a combination of toddler and teenager, was gone. And if the state of his garden was any indication, Aakash now needed Esme as much as she needed him. It was intimidating to feel needed by him. But it was nice, too.

After he went up to bed, she went outside and watered each and every one of his plants. Then she lay on her back in the cool grass, like she hadn't done since she was a child, and stared up at the silent stars she could never see in the sky over Philly. Their brilliance lit up the growing darkness around her and bathed her in something like hope.

**

Two days later, Esme strode into the living room and turned off the TV over her father's indignant protests. She perched herself on the coffee table across from him. "Dad, I know about Mom. Ambika told me. Why haven't you talked to me about this?"

Aakash's surprise looked genuine. "You're having your own troubles right now, Esme. I didn't want to burden you with mine."

"Well, I want you to. Lay it on me. Did she even give you a reason?"

"Oh, who knows with your mother." Aakash started to reach for the remote, but Esme tossed it onto the couch out of his reach.

"Dad, please. You can talk to me. Why won't you just talk to me?"

He stared at her hard like he wasn't going to break, but then his shoulders sagged, and she could see the words building inside of him just before they came rushing out. "It's all this new-age modern stuff about not being happy," he said. "Back home, she'd have never left me for a reason like that. I don't raise my voice or my hand to her. I worked hard to support her and my children. I've never been addicted to anything. I'm in bed beside her each night—no affairs. But none of that is enough anymore." He shook his head. "I think she even used the word fulfilled in there. I don't make her feel fulfilled." He laughed even though it wasn't funny.

"It's not silly that she wants to be happy, Dad. That she wants you to at least care if she is or not."

"Don't think I didn't know you'd be on her side." He rubbed his chin. "I always thought we'd go back, you know, once you kids were all grown up. To India. Your mother—she never wanted to. But I thought maybe that would change. She'd start to remember where we came from and stop feeling like she had to be ashamed of it. But no. This place is home to her now. Not there. Not me." He smiled at Esme. "I've never quite fit here myself."

"You really were going to go back there? And leave us?"

"After retiring, sure. Once you girls didn't need us anymore. Once you were self-sufficient. Not that I could have yet." He gestured at Esme. "What would become of you if I did?"

"I'd get by." They both laughed now. "Dad, have you at least tried to call her? Talk to her? Can't you go there? Show her that you give a crap enough to listen and work on making things better together?"

He stood up and retrieved the remote. He dropped back down in his chair. "She just needs to get this out of her system. And if she doesn't want to come back, then let her go be happy. Whatever that is."

When Matthew texted Esme a few hours later to ask when she'd be back in town, she wrote, "This isn't working for me anymore. Sorry," and hit send before she could second guess it. She went outside with the jasmine plant she'd gotten from a local nursery earlier, grabbing her father's fat orange gloves on the way out. She knelt down and transferred it into the soft soil that she'd layered with compost and patted it in with a gentle resolve completely foreign to her.

**

The next few days drifted by without much conversation of note. On their quietest night, the two managed to make it through an entire meal exchanging nothing more than a nod before going to bed. She almost began to miss the sound of his lectures and considered complaining about her life to bring one on. In the morning, Esme awoke to the sound of her father shouting her name from downstairs. The last time he'd done that, she'd been a teenager oversleeping and making them late for temple. There was an urgent quality to his voice that was familiar, but also a tinge of wonder that was less so. Rubbing her eyes and cursing internally, she willed herself out of bed and onto her feet before staggering down the stairs.

"Dad, what the hell is it? Are you okay?" She looked around, unable to locate him through the sleepy blur in her vision.

"Come. You have to see this." He was at the back door, waving her over, and then he disappeared. She joined him out in his garden, just as she had on the first day she arrived.

"Look, Easwari. My flowers. I know I haven't been good about tending to them, but they're thriving on their own. Look at the color of those begonias. I'm not one to talk of miracles, but I guess a little patience and time was all they needed. Nature knows what it's doing, right?"

"Right." Esme wouldn't dream of embarrassing him now with the correction that she was the one who had been safeguarding his darlings in his absence. Not when the look of elation on his face was one she'd never seen before.

Aakash turned to face her, and they held the eye contact they usually found so disconcerting and avoided at any cost. He remained difficult to read, but it felt like he was really seeing her. Like he knew it was her that had taken care of him without her needing to say it. He looked back at his blossoming lilies and perky peonies and squeezed her shoulder. She waited, sure he was going to say something. She didn't know what it was, but she wanted it more than anything. His smile was a thin line, but it was there. He was heading back inside before she fully registered that the moment had come and gone. But it had come.

She followed him into the house after a few minutes. When she reached the top of the staircase, she saw his door ajar and peeked in. A small carry-on bag was open on the bed with a few shirts and pants haphazardly spread out beside it. Just enough for a short trip to Mimi Auntie's. Esme could hear him rustling around in his closet and hastened away before he could catch her there.

After making herself appear and feel more human, Esme wandered back out to the garden. The rays of the rising sun warmed her skin. She made her way over to the jasmine flowers, their strong fragrance waking her all the way up before she even saw them. Waxy and white, small but clustered together into a larger whole, the bright buds appeared on the cusp of opening and blooming fully. Any lingering tension in her bones, from the time spent waiting for her father's words that would not come, thawed and softened in their presence. She promised herself that later, she'd respond to the request for an interview she'd received in an e-mail the night before. It wasn't a dream job, but it was something. She didn't know exactly what she wanted from her life next, but this seemed as fine a spot as any to sit and think.

Tape and Glue

"Who's your mother taking up with now?" My father's voice is much too nonchalant, betraying how easily my answer could actually break him.

I honestly don't mind if it does. I would lose no sleep if I were responsible for that. It'd be no worse than what he's done to my mother over the years, trampling all over her trust and dignity more times than I care to count. Left it to my brothers and me to fix her up every time. We've dressed her in so much uneven, peeling tape and smeared her with so many globs of sticky glue, but the damage can still be seen underneath. It gets hard to keep it all smooth, without the bumps and ridges, when the task arises so often. We partly want everything he's put her through to show, too. We feel some pride in how she always manages to overcome her seemingly insurmountable heartache. Leaving her blemish free to keep up appearances might have saved her some unwanted attention and gossip, but it would have papered over her strength, too. My mother's strength is my strength, so I wave it like a flag for her, whether she wants me to or not.

My father is driving so fast over the speed limit now, like always, that I can feel the indents of my fingernails in my palms and the tightness in my jaw from grinding my teeth the whole time. He asks again, "Did you hear me, Sita? What bozo is she seeing now?"

I let Dad wait a bit, enjoying his refusal to squirm though I know his insides are. It almost gives me a perverse pleasure now to serve up and hit him with the response he's dreading. My conversations with my father are tennis matches, slow to build up but long and grueling. They can take us well into the night, the sweat streaming down our faces, our backs aching with the prolonged strain. Our shared talent in tennis, both the actual sport and the linguistic kind, is about all we have in common anymore. But we do love us some tennis.

"Oh, this one? This one's different. You know Mom and her series of tests, but he passed them all. They're in it for real. Maybe I'll be a bridesmaid. It'd be my first time, you know." I've hurt him, but he refuses to concede the point, lobbing the fuzzy green ball right at me.

"She's got better friends than you to stand up there with her. Besides, your mother doesn't tolerate much. She doesn't weather storms too well. Lacks staying power. Let them have a first fight. I wouldn't buy the dress just yet."

My racket echoes like a cannon upon impact as I slam the ball before it can pass me, sending it hurtling back toward him. "I'd say the problem's always been with her taste, not with her patience for bull. She chooses wrong sometimes, but now she finally knows how to get out of there once she realizes it." My smile of victory is almost too much for him to bear as my shot hits its mark, sailing past him and bouncing just inside the line out of his reach.

"Well good. I'm happy for her. I'm glad you like him, too, Sita." He clears his throat too many times as we merge onto the highway.

As always, no matter how much he deserves it, I feel a little guilty after a win like that. No one really likes the feeling of beating their father.

**

I'm the only one that still spends every other weekend and the summer with him at his sad little apartment. Neil and Dev were already in med school and college by the time Mom said she had finally had enough and made Dad move out. He's lucky if my brothers force themselves to visit him once every several months.

We all had started to get the impression that Mom didn't know how to do such a thing as call a lawyer and do something so official, legal, and public as file for divorce. But she did know, and she did do it. Sometimes I wonder—and feel so disloyal to wonder—if she could stagger through all those heartbreaking and humiliating episodes of infidelity but stay with him for the sake of my brothers, to allow them to wrap up their childhoods with the illusion of happy family intact whenever they felt like ignoring our reality, then why not for me? Why did she make me become a child of divorce all by myself without my brothers for company?

I like to think I know why. I like to think it's exactly because I'm not her son. I'm her only daughter. She didn't want her staying with Dad to be the example she set for me—a lesson that would have been hard to make me unlearn. She couldn't let me leave home for good, thinking that it's a woman's job to suffer and bear the ultimate betrayal and disrespect, not once, not twice, but over and over. All in the name of loyalty and family. I'm proud of her for ending it, and I tell her so. Often. Whenever I can tell she misses him.

Not too many of the other Indians we know in our small but predominantly Indian immigrant community in Fremont, California come from broken homes like ours. Plenty grew up in and survived unhappy homes, sure. Some worse than our situation, if I'm being honest. Splitting up would have done a few of their families far greater good than the admirable act of hanging in there, shackled to each other for life with plastic, grinning grimaces frozen in photos as evidence. Most of our neighbors and acquaintances from temple wear their hard-won longevity like badges. I'm sure it isn't that none of them have ever fantasized about straying, but it's incredibly rare for any to have ever acted on it. My dad, though, he's one of a kind. A real maverick, not held back by tradition, convention, or the horrified whispers behind our backs at social gatherings.

Sometimes my mom would say that we're all too hard on him. That he didn't let the total poverty and lack of education that were his family's fate in India define him. That he fled with mere dollars in his pocket and my mother around his neck, promising her that their children would never want for anything and then following through on that vow. That the life he made possible for all of us here through his own sheer will and determination isn't something to disregard for the sake of our woe is me narrative. That he's been warm, loving, and patient with us all our lives and has always immersed himself in anything we ever cared about, unlike the many distant and detached fathers we know in our circle.

"A dad who struggles to keep his pants on in the company of other women isn't as bad as a dad who beats you or starves you with his own laziness and fondness for drink," she'd remind us. She told us that's what our grandfather did to Dad and his siblings in the dark, dirty hovel they had to call home, squandering what little scraps they had on booze and pulling out his belt at the slightest provocation. "You kids take your father for granted," she'd argue each time she walked in on one of our many bash Dad fests. They ranged in gravity as we discussed how he and his shenanigans were to blame for the C we got on that test, the goal we didn't score in that one game, or the chances in love we'll now never be brave enough to take. Mom was not impressed. Neil's degree in psychology and eloquence were no match for her scathing impatience with our feelings.

"If only our problems back home then were as trivial as yours are here now. Then we could find all this nonsense to complain about, too. If your greatest obstacle is a father with a wandering eye—"

"He lets a lot more than his eye wander!" it would inevitably be my turn to chime in.

"If that's the worst you've got," she'd continue loudly, "then you're going to have to toughen up. No one will care about that once you're out in the world, expected to fly on your own merit."

"Well, then it's your fault for making life too easy for us that a little thing like our father cheating on our mother, oh I don't know, bothers us?" Dev's gentle voice always took the sting out of such pointed accusations.

"Feel free not to eat the food your father puts on the table or wear the clothes he puts on your backs. And forget about those fancy schools he funds with his retirement money. You'll all be a lovely trio of hungry, naked fools with no diplomas. You'll be excusing his misdeeds before long."

"Is that why you stay?" is the question the three of us never asked her.

She's been less vocal about defending him since the divorce, understandably, but every once in a while, she'll still offer a halfhearted, "Oh, give the guy a break."

**

Dad and I have arrived at his place for the weekend. As he drags my luggage up the rickety outdoor staircase, thudding over each step, he calls out like he does every time I visit, "I really need to find an apartment with an elevator."

"Yeah, Dad, I know. So you've said. About eighty times." My eye roll and heavy dose of attitude are a bit too stereotypically teenage girl for my taste, but I can't be original all the time.

He forces a laugh coupled with a grunt as he almost trips up the last few stairs. "I guess I still say it because you still haven't gotten the hint. Either bring less stuff or just start leaving some here that would be waiting for you each time."

I wrinkle my nose and shake my head.

"Well, sorry for that suggestion—just thought it would make sense since this is your home, too. Not some hotel you frequent."

I laugh dryly. "This is certainly not a hotel I'd choose voluntarily."

"Sita—"

"I know Mom got to keep the house, but she's not the type who bled you dry. You could afford better than this, right?"

"I'm sorry I've raised you to think that way. I meant to teach you better values. Saving for the future is what I do. Saving is how we got that house in the first place and how you attend that prep school. So I'm not going to get some quartz countertops and stainless steel appliances just to mimic the life I gave up. I can make do like this, so I can keep saving for you kids and the kids you'll have someday."

"Dad, jeez, relax. I'm not such a princess. I just meant you can afford a place with an elevator and a few more drawers for my stuff. And it's hardly home if my room when I stay here is really yours and you just sleep on the couch."

He sets my bags down on the stained concrete walkway and ignores all the chipped paint, peeled off siding, and the general dilapidated state of everything that makes it feel like Norman Bates will be by any minute to check how we like our room. Dad then heaves with all his might and yanks open the misshapen door, forever stuck and never repaired from repeated earthquake damage. Together, we survey the tiny apartment, his sacrifice now filling me with discomfort. He does always say he plans to contribute to the down payment on all three of our first homes, but my brothers write it off as guilt money.

"Sita, some families of our size all live in one or two bedroom apartments together their whole lives, even when their kids get married and start having kids of their own. They all make it work because family is more important than space. You never had to live like that, but your brothers did when we first came to this country. We lived in a two bedroom apartment, all four of us, with my brother that sponsored us and his wife and daughter. Neil and Dev just don't remember. They had a lot of fun and happy memories in that apartment, and it was no palace."

"If space is so overrated, then you probably shouldn't have purchased a mini mansion where we all got our own rooms, a guest room, and a home theatre. And then expected us to learn that all that stuff isn't necessary through osmosis. This is just a big adjustment for me, that's all. I'm trying to get used to it. I really am. I just like a little more privacy for me and my things. Sorry if that makes me a selfish brat."

He nods. "Okay, okay, fair point. I'll look into adding some more furniture for you, but I'm afraid the sleeping arrangement is what it is for now."

I'm proud of myself for withholding my other fair point—that if family is so much more valuable than space, it's probably beneficial to control your animalistic urges around outsiders. I still feel crappy, though, even having not said it.

Later, while we're eating Thai takeout for lunch in front of the TV, Dad says, "So I've got a proposition for you."

I glance up from my red curry, wary and suspicious. "I won't help you get Mom back if that's where this is headed."

"God, Sita, you can be so—When have I ever asked you to do that? No, this isn't about me and your mother. What do you say to a road trip this summer when school's over? Just you and me? You'll have your permit, so you can get some practice driving, too. We can just meander up and down the coast if you want—plenty to do and see—or check out the middle of the country you've never set foot in yet. Well? Go ahead. First thoughts. Hit me."

The truth is if he'd asked me five years earlier to be alone in a car with him for days on end, I'd be jumping up and down. I'd already be imagining us singing an eclectic mixture of his favorite classic rock like The Eagles, blended with our guilty pleasure Bollywood staples like *Kuch Kuch Hota Hai*, all at the top of our lungs with the windows down. We'd take breaks only to roast marshmallows together under a soft watercolor sky in Big Sur, overlooking the endless ocean and purple mountains, or to try our luck on surfboards in the clear blue waves of Malibu that twinkle and sparkle in the sunlight. My dad was my whole world back then. I thought he painted the earth himself, streaking and glittering it with the moon and stars just for me. I certainly never thought him capable of hurting my mother and destroying our family.

But you can't go backward. I can't unknow what I now know. I can't unexperience all of it. So, "No. No thanks, Dad. I'm sorry."

He sees his tennis ball has hit the net and bounced back to him, its movement sluggish and weak. That swift a rejection can't have felt good. But like a true professional, he shakes it off and keeps going like nothing happened.

"Well, I hoped you'd at least give it some thought, but, hey, it's up to you, kiddo." He goes to clear our plates off in the kitchen sink, and I look out the window. It's a dreary scene at this sea green motel looking place. I can't keep winning all our match points like this. You hit a certain age where, no matter how flawed your parents turn out to be, it still feels pretty depressing to see them hurting and know you did it to them.

**

It was a few months earlier that my father caught me smoking just outside the woods bordering his apartment complex. As a smoker who started as a teenager himself, he chewed me out pretty good. It was annoying and hypocritical to say the least. I pointed that out, as well as threatening not to come stay with him anymore if he told Mom. Laid on a lot of guilt, blame, and emotional warfare about his affairs and his smoking my whole life—you know—attacking the "do as I say, not as I do" deal. I felt lousy doing it, but I also like smoking. Getting to do it with a bit less subterfuge every other weekend is a nice break from life with Mom, who can resemble a prison warden when she wants to. When it comes to homework, studying, boys, and, well, not smoking, she is an intense nag—and an effective one.

Once I had my Dad where I wanted him, he came around to me smoking. He didn't like it at first, but each visit, it became one more thing to bring us together, however tenuous and temporary the connection. We get to forget everything else and enjoy the closeness unique to smokers indulging in their shameful habit in secret together.

So after we return to the apartment from dinner at my uncle's house, Dad and I realize he is down to just one or two Camel Turkish Silvers—we like how they've got blue stripes and are "Turkish". Makes us feel very worldly. He offers to go pick them up for us, and that works for me, since I wouldn't mind some alone time to unwind from our awkward avoidance of the failed road trip idea..

After he's been gone about ten minutes or so, there's a knock on the door. I can be a paranoid person, especially as a teenage girl alone in an unfamiliar place that will never be home. Dad has plenty of neighbors around. Still, I'm not too thrilled to have someone unexpected show up. I go and stand on my tiptoes to glance out the peephole. Whoever this lady is, she's not short like me. I'm pretty much looking at her chest instead of her face, so makes it hard to identify her.

She knocks again, causing me to fall back on my heels. "You in there? It's me." She doesn't sound dangerous at all, and my curiosity gets the better of me.

I pull the door open part way and look her up and down. She's attractive. She smiles too much for a stranger showing up unannounced. I don't like it.

"Who are you?" I ask.

"I'm Nancy. And who are you?"

"I'm asking the questions. I live here, not you." Well, this is escalating quickly, mostly on my part. But I know why my cheeks are hot, my palms slick with angry sweat, and my tone confrontational. She is sleeping with my father. I can just tell. The decades my strong and aging gracefully mother has on her, as well as her too fit body and long blonde hair, make my heart drum against my chest.

"Live here? Excuse me. AJ is my boyfriend." She takes a step closer, and it strikes me again just how much taller than me she is.

"Yeah? Well, Abhijit is my dad." Trust Dad to dust off and pull out his old Americanized nickname for this girl.

"Oh! Sita, I'm so sorry. I've been looking forward to meeting you. I just didn't know you'd be here tonight. I was in the neighborhood, so I thought I'd drop by and check on—"

"He's told you about me?" This makes me physically sick. What is this? She's barely older than I am. She thinks this is a bonafide relationship? Does Dad think so, too? Or does he just make her think so? I might even feel sorry for her if that is the case.

"Well, sure. I know about all of you—Neil and Dev are all grown up, but you're still in high school."

"All grown up? I'm pretty sure they're both older than you which, frankly, is gross."

"That's pretty judgmental," she says. "Can we start over?"

"Okay, so you know our names. Good for you. No, really, congrats. I suppose that means you know about Leela?"

She tenses and takes a step back from me, still on the other side of the doorway. I will not let her pass me. I guard the gate in this moment and will be my father's chastity belt against this child who is probably just seeking his money for treats and trinkets anyway.

"Sita, your parents are divorced. Your father will always love your mother, but they are not together anymore."

"He's old enough to be your father."

"Don't be rude."

"Not rude," I tell her. "Just a statement of fact. If you don't want people to accuse you of grave robbing, don't engage in behavior that literally matches the definition."

"That's an awfully morbid thing to say."

"So I like my humor dark. You're not my mom. I can say whatever I want." I avoid the urge to cross my arms over my chest and pout like a defiant toddler.

"You certainly can. Just startled me. You're his daughter, so it's pretty insensitive, that's all, given the circumstances."

"What circumstances?"

"You know," she says. "The diagnosis."

The ball hits me square in the stomach, the air rushing and billowing out of my mouth in a comical O shape. Only Dad can best me in tennis when he's not even there. When I don't even know that we're playing. My eyebrows furrowed, I wonder if she's messing with me. To get back at me for giving her a hard time.

"What the hell are you talking about?"

"He's sick." She sees my blank stare. "Kidney cancer. He could die. C'mon, I'm not telling you anything you don't already know. He found out weeks ago and said he was going to go see you the next day."

I refuse to hand her the triumph of knowing she is more savvy to my father's most serious of health scares than I am. "Of course I know. I just am surprised you do. Usually in a meaningless fling, that sort of subject doesn't make for the best pillow talk. And that's what you are to him. Meaningless."

"Sita—"

"I think you should go now."

She hesitates for a minute and I can tell she's trying to peer over my shoulder, to see if her beloved AJ is at home in the shoebox living room, listening but not defending her. I start to close the door, letting it nudge her sandals out of my way. She's halfway down the outdoor hallway before the bricks that have been waiting patiently for our back and forth to conclude come tumbling down on me, crushing me with the unfeeling weight of their truth. Kidney cancer.

I close the door and grope around for a chair in the sparse room, finally sitting down and letting myself crumble and cry like the little Daddy's girl I haven't been for so long now. It feels like ages before his keys jangle outside and the front door creaks back open. I stand up, ready for our most epic volley of all.

"Here." He tosses the fresh box of cigarettes at me and looks surprised when it hits the ground. "Forget how to catch?"

"Cancer, Dad?"

I expect him to freeze or move in slow-mo or any of the clichés one is described as doing in those tensest of moments like this one. Instead he walks over to the cigs, picks them up, and places them on the table. We're both silent for a few minutes, contemplating our next move.

Finally, "I guess Nancy stopped by, huh?"

"Were you ever planning on telling me? Your Prom Date Barbie knows before I do?"

"Let's cool it with the theatrics and drama queen level of exaggeration. Nancy's almost twenty-eight. We met in a club for hiking enthusiasts."

"Ha!" My voice is dripping with sarcasm intended to wound. "Our poor father, the outdoorsman whose family held him back from exploring his true passions all these years. Thank god you found Nancy to help you reinvent yourself. She's who you should take on your stupid road trip."

"Sita, I understand, okay? You're allowed to lash out usually. I've messed up royally and let you down a lot. Believe me, I know. But this is different. Of course I was going to tell you. This was it. Me telling you. This weekend."

"Real nice to have your girlfriend do it for you." The more I feel like crying, the angrier at him I become.

"Would you settle down and cut me some slack?" Uniquely American expressions still always sound funny and wrong to me in my dad's accent, no matter how long he's lived here and used them. "Obviously, I didn't plan for you to hear it from her. I didn't even know she'd show up here. I just stepped out to get us some more cigs like you wanted. It's not my fault she dropped in on you." His voice is uncharacteristically rising in volume now. "Not everything is on me dammit." I'm not responding or egging him on, like we usually do to each other, but that only seems to be goading him more. "This thing, this one thing, you can't blame on me. It's not my fault. You don't get to make it my fault that I'm sick and didn't tell you the right way. There is no right way." He drops down into a chair and looks at the ground, defeated. I feel about as bad as I'm capable of feeling for him.

"Easy, Dad. You're right. Okay? You're right. Sorry."

"Thanks."

We zip up our rackets into their cases and shake hands over the net dividing us.

"Let's go back a step. You're sick? How serious? She made it sound like you're dying."

"Pretty damn serious unfortunately. Not as dire as Prom Date Barbie made it sound though." He shoots me a smile, rueful but conspiratorial. "I'm not dying, I don't think. Or I will, but not next month anyway."

"Yeah, I mean I didn't get the impression you were with her for her stellar intellect." We're both smiling now.

"Conversations with any wit or nuance have been hard to come by, it's true. It's my fault for telling her. She's a bit literal. So according to her, I'm a goner any day now."

"How will you break the bad news to her that she might not be a bountiful widow as soon as she thought?"

"I didn't want to disappoint her with the revelation that we might not still be dating by the time I make a final draft of my will. Better we enjoy our brief time in the sun together without that looming over our heads. Life's too short after all." All of a sudden, things feel kind of heavy again.

I slice a backhand his way, but one I know he can get to in time. "Yeah, especially hers. There's only been like eighteen years of it so far."

"Hey! Nineteen."

It feels nice to make fun of her together for a little while. A light distraction. It helps.

"Have you told Dev or Neil yet?"

"Nah. Figured you deserve some special points for being the only one who still lives here sometimes. Even if it's because you're a minor and you have to."

I think about Mom finally starting to move on and Dad knowing he'll have to forever regret what he did to her and our family now that he's facing his own mortality. I think about how he's facing it pretty alone. I think about how my brothers and I always tended to Mom's wounds that he caused and never much cared about his, the ones he got long before we were ever born. I think about how I've made mistakes, but Mom forgives me. And how I'll keep making them, and I hope she keeps forgiving me.

"Oh, I don't know. It's not so bad here. Maybe I've forgotten to tell them that."

"Don't go getting sentimental on me now. I don't recognize you. You're creeping me out." Yet another turn of phrase that sounds so awkward coming from his mouth.

"Yeah I don't like it either. But let's maybe do that road trip. Could be fun. As long as you don't pick up any dates half your age on the way."

"I'll try not to."

"Where do you want to go?"

"Wherever the spirit of adventure takes us. As long as we sleep under the moon and stars just once, I can die happy."

I want to pretend I'm eleven again and he's the best dad in the world. For now, I decide to hold that image together with some tape and glue.

"Well if that's all it'll take, I guess I can do that. Just once."

He opens the pack, pulls a cigarette out, and reaches over to hand it to me. I wait while he gets one for himself. We both light up at the same time, and I take a long drag with my young, full lungs. His is a lot shorter from a lifetime of doing it.

"Dad, I'm still pretty mad at you. This doesn't change that."

"I know."

"But we can table it until you're better."

"Sure," he says, taking a slightly longer drag. "We've got some time."

Look Where We're Going

Nina had informed him of the unplanned pregnancy that morning, as casually as she was now asking him to admire her appearance. She spun away from enjoying her reflection in the mirror to face him. She spread her arms and twitched her hips. "How do I look?"

Amol observed his light haired, light eyed girlfriend—dressed in an Indian sari and covered in ostentatious gold jewelry—with a mixture of pride and amusement. She looked wonderful and yet wrong at the same time. Like an excited young girl playing dress up. So precious, but not real.

"You look amazing." He sat down on the bed they shared most nights in his modestly sized Manhattan apartment. Nina described the color on the walls as a drab and dependable gray without being asked. The blanket on the bed was black, and Nina's sari in front of him was an electric blend of pinks, yellows, and greens.

"Your sister taught me how to drape and pin the sari last week. I did okay?"

He smiled. "Better than some Indian women I know."

"Give me a break." She returned to the mirror, putting the final touches on her appearance and applying a ruby red to her pale lips.

He stood up to find sandals to complement his long beige kurta. They were headed to his cousin's Hindu wedding in Connecticut. Nina tossed her lipstick onto the bed. Irritated, he picked it up and walked over to the vanity to return it to its place.

"We should get on the road now. Don't want to be late."

Amol knew he was kidding himself. With Nina coming along, of course they'd be late. Amol's mother, with her quiet dignity and grace, believed beyond a shadow of a doubt that loud, cursing, irresponsible Nina was nothing but a fling. Something Amol had to get out of his system. Amol's mother knew her meticulous son needed someone who would drop her clothes in the laundry hamper in the evening. Not step out of her pants and skirts, leaving them discarded on the floor like some kind of helpful chalk outline to aid him in tracing her last steps. He needed someone who would understand and respect their Hindu customs and beliefs. Not try them on like a costume when it suited her. Someone he could actually take to temple and family gatherings with no sense of dread that he was teetering on the edge, about to make one wrong move and plummet. The girl didn't have to be brown, his mother insisted. She just couldn't be Nina.

Amol, even as he rebelled for the first time and resisted his mother, wondered if she was right. The baby made it all so much more troubling somehow. What if this unpredictable life of his was simply a precursor to the one yet to happen?

Thanks to Nina, he'd found himself on a flight to Greece in only their third week of dating because she was just really into her new Mediterranean cookbook and wanted to see the birthplace of it all. It was at her insistence that they woke up in the dead of night once to go ride their bikes through a pitch black Central Park in the winter. Amol could still remember how the cold had seized every muscle of his body until they screamed and ached, and then the exhilarating release when the wind whistling in his ears and the crunch of the white frost beneath his wheels made him laugh. Without Nina, he would have ordered takeout from the little Greek hole in the wall down the street or just exercised on the bike machine at his gym under the warm, comfortable glow of a heater.

He tried to picture the steady, reliable partner he hadn't met yet, but she had no face. And yet a part of him still wanted her. Was waiting for her.

Assumed they'd find each other someday. Then Nina's chatter in the car paused.

"You're too quiet. What's wrong?"

Amol was surprised Nina noticed.

"It's the baby."

"I knew it." She was trying to catch his eye—he could tell—but he avoided her penetrating gaze. The road stretching long and unknown in front of him was all he could see.

"I have to look where I'm going." He felt her pressing up against his arm as he drove on without turning to face her, the gold chain of her elaborate, chunky necklace leaving an uncomfortable indent in his skin through his thin sleeve.

"We can do this," she said.

"I—I don't want to."

The next few moments felt gaping and cold. The gray seatbelt cut into his flesh. Darkness had fallen. They were almost at the wedding venue.

"I wasn't expecting this." He released the steering wheel, hot from his tight grip and cold from his sweat, and reached out to rest his hand on her knee. The fabric of her sari felt scratchy and thick to his touch.

She shifted her knee so that his hand dropped to her seat.

He turned back to the road in time to see the deer, a light brown blur, dart out in front of the car. He jerked the wheel with both hands, and his eyes widened as the world spun into a dizzying shock of colors in the heavy darkness.

Once his brain started whirring again and sensation surged through his body, Amol became aware that he was alive. Nina's hand touched his face.

"We're alright," she said. "We're okay. So is the deer."

Amol rolled the window down. He felt the pressure in his head and lungs lessen as the cold air rushed in and he laughed. The sound circled him and Nina both, banding them together tighter and tighter, until they could hardly breathe. Her teeth scraped his cheekbone as her kisses attacked him, hungry and wanting. He closed his eyes and listened. All he could hear was the violent beating of their three hearts.

Long Distance Loyalty

Engaged. Another one. Nothing in the realm of reason or fairness could explain the four young women in Jenny's class all receiving proposals one after another. If it had been anything to do with their shared major, then maybe she would be engaged, too. Studying journalism in graduate school didn't seem to be the elusive formula, at least not in Jenny's case.

Probably it was her boyfriend. Mark. She wasn't dating the type of guy whose first priority was getting married. They weren't even close to moving in together. The bedroom door swung open, interrupting her thought process.

"Sorry, I'm here finally. What's up?" She looked up to see her tardy companion enter. He ran a tanned hand through his dark hair. He crawled into the bed beside her, punching the pillow. It took her a moment to even register that he was speaking to her.

Would Mark ever drop down on one knee, the independent free spirit that he was? He'd been romantic at the beginning, and there was little doubt that he was committed to her and faithful. He was affectionate when they were together. Yes, he was all those things. Jenny couldn't pretend that Mark wasn't a good man.

"Hello, you hear me?" Her back was to him, so he tapped her on the shoulder. She turned over on her side to face him, a forced smile on her lips.

"No, I must have spaced out. Long day."

"You seemed out of it. How's that article you're working on?"

"Not bad. I might have you take a look at it later." She leaned in and kissed him on the forehead.

"Sure, no problem."

"I'll be right back." As she swung her legs over the side of the bed, she turned back to ruffle his black curls.

Once alone in front of the bathroom mirror, she began brushing her teeth and returned to her earlier concerns. Would Mark come to his senses and realize that they were adults now, surrounded by other adults, and that all of them were getting married? No, Mark wouldn't notice. He would only notice that the Earth was getting warmer, certain species were going extinct, and too many children in the world didn't have enough to eat. His beliefs and causes were always taking him to the far reaches of the planet, away from Philadelphia and away from her. How was Mark going to find the time to realize what a fabulous wife she'd make when he was constantly boarding planes to write about injustices in remote villages?

She spat her blue toothpaste into the sink too soon with a surge of violence. She tried to wipe the sticky blob away with her finger, streaking it across the white porcelain in a zigzag. She ran warm water over it, but the stain remained.

She returned to the dimly lit bedroom to find him on his stomach and propped up on his elbows, reading.

Closing the book, he heaved a dramatic sigh. "Listen, I got some weird news today. Martha called me."

"And what did she want?"

"She and Tim—they're having a baby. She wanted to make sure I heard it from her."

Jenny slung one leg over his waist and sat up, placing her weight on the small of his back. She began rubbing his tight shoulders. "I'm sorry. It does seem like everything in their relationship has moved pretty fast."

"It has! But I don't care. Or I shouldn't. It's been two years already since she left me for him. Jeez, I'm an ass. You probably don't want to hear about this."

"No, really, I don't mind."

"Thanks, Jen. You're sweet."

This comment made her mind wander again. Maybe that was the problem—she was a far too giving and supportive person. Why should Mark need to marry her? He was already getting all the wifely treatment without it.

"Come here." He shifted so that she'd have to climb down from his back. He turned over and pulled her on top of his chest until their noses were almost touching. "I'd rather focus on you now than think about pregnant Martha."

"Probably a very nauseous pregnant Martha."

He laughed. "See? You're just the best."

Her attention now solely on the attractive face and light brown eyes in front of her, she began kissing and undressing him. He flipped her onto her back. His breath on her neck was hot and hungry and his knees parting her legs were confident and sure. After, she curled up and fit snugly into the shape created by his curved figure behind her.

She was a good person, even if she wasn't daily trying to save the world like Mark. Her life was meaningful, too. He couldn't look down on her just because she wasn't protesting and shouting in the streets surrounded by the people, grasping their hands, and then scribbling the inhumanity of their situation down on paper.

She'd be a trustworthy news anchor for the people of Philly. She'd be a devoted mother and a loyal wife. What more could Mark want? How many more engaged journalists could she bear to congratulate? And yet, she'd understood early on that the man she was falling for was not the settle down and cuddle on the couch type. Mark was a selfless and noble crusader. Loving him meant accepting he'd often not be there. She'd known that.

She snuggled in closer to the strong, hard body beside her, breathing in the warmth he radiated. Her cell phone began vibrating atop the nightstand. She sat up. He looked at her, a little nervous.

"Who's that calling? It's kind of late."

She saw the image of sandy haired, blue eyed Mark smiling at her from the phone's lit up display screen. The knots in her stomach returned. "Dammit. It's my boyfriend. Be quiet while I answer. It must be daytime wherever he is in Asia."

Tomorrow

One day the woman wakes up and she can't say exactly what it is that's changed, only that she knows it all has.

Then she looks around.

Outside the window, there is the street and trees and houses she knows, but there is also water she doesn't. Great big dark waves, some crashing, some lilting and lapping, some loud and angry, some gentle and soft, but all grand in its music.

The floor beside her bed is still cherry hardwood like it was yesterday— or at least she thinks it is anyway—not oatmeal colored carpet like when she'd first moved in to the place. But it also might not be. It could be that it's neither of those things. It's possibly vast and endless and not even there at all. It could be swirling black and gray and white and infinite, pouring down like milk through a funnel, opening up at the base to a sky of stars below.

She could just stay in bed, safe from all the dangers surrounding her, or she could explore the unknown.

So she drifts her way outside, letting the wind carry her there. She's sort of flying, sort of not. She glides along the water, and soon she's not alone. There are people and animals she likes and people and animals she doesn't, and she's glad for once not to be in the solitude of her home.

Her neighbors and friends and old lovers and missed connections and boss from her job she hates and that one girl that bullied her decades ago in school and that boy that kissed and touched her without asking or caring if it was okay and the man she'd fallen deeply and completely in love with who liked her just fine but not in the same way or with the depth of emotion she felt for him and the woman from work she had hurt very badly with the gossip she spread about her and the dog who had bitten the bicyclist and the dog who strangers loved to pet at the park and finally a new man she's not known for very long but who catches her eye and her attention in a way that flutters pleasurably and almost painfully deep inside her belly— they are all there, too.

Further along, where the street ends—or just beyond it, rather—are oceans and mountains and ice and snow and sun and rain and the rest of the world and their joy and pain and war and hunger and hurting and happiness and it all feels unbearably far and close all at once. She reaches her hands out, but though she can see it all, she can't touch it. So she breathes in her disappointment, puts on a smile, and focuses instead on these faces surrounding her from the town she knows but doesn't recognize today.

Hello, they say. But the new man says it in a tone that is meaningful and distinct from the others, and when they look at each other, their gazes fuse in a way that makes everyone else know to float away and give them some privacy.

As their bodies intertwine beneath the blankets on her bed, his head finds the normally empty and unused second pillow. He creates a comfortable shape for himself in it, a groove within which he can fit for all the days to come. In that moment, his warmth and her warmth meet. Visible sparks start to fly and ignite an actual fire. She is startled but doesn't dare move away from him. The flames are more white and gold and blue than she would have thought, not so red and orange as she'd been taught to expect. The flames should scare her—they are catching fast—but the heat is so pleasant and cozy that she is not afraid of burning—she is afraid of how it would feel for it all to go away with him, for his body and the fire to be gone, and for everything to be cold again, including her. Especially her. She'd be safe, but his pillow would be empty and cool, and she can't have that. She concludes, yes, I want the fire, if it means I can have him and me. Together.

She knows this whole thing is half rendered and surreal like a dream, but it also feels real, realer than anything she's lived through yet. She wants to trust it but isn't sure.

Go to sleep, he breathes into her ear.

Her skin is starting to smell like bread she's left too long in the toaster, and her nerves tingle now with something more than happiness. She can almost feel the pain of the fire grazing her bare arms.

Good night, he says. Then he pulls her in close, showering them both with even more sparks that sing and flicker like stars.

In the morning, she looks out the window and there is no water. She leans over the edge of her bed to see that the floor is just a floor. Her bedroom and home are not a charred skeleton. Everything is the same as it was before.

Until she hears a loud creaking noise and sees the doorknob across the room begin to turn as if by itself, as if by magic. Someone must be on the other side of the door, but she lives alone, and so she remembers to be frightened as well as curious.

Before she can ask who is there, the door opens. It is the man, and he is holding two mugs of coffee.

You're awake! Sorry if I was too loud in the kitchen, he says. But now that you're up, join me?

Yes, I will, she says. Thank you.

She follows him down the hall, memorizing the rhythm of his steps and timing the beats of hers to harmonize with his. The floor under her feet is hard and cold, but she is on fire.

You're Still You

My earlobes were the first thing I touched after waking from the brief coma caused by the accident. I was glad I could rub them between my fingers, unharmed and unbloodied—so different from the rest of what remained of my face. It was comforting and cozy to pinch and pull on them like saltwater taffy when surrounded by the doctors discussing me and my case each morning during rounds. I could hear with my ears and also escape into the texture of them.

Reconstruction makes you as unrecognizable to yourself as anyone else. They wanted to prepare me for what that first look in the mirror would be like after the surgery. They didn't believe I was excited. You should be proud, I told them, not afraid to reveal your intricate and elaborate work. I joked to the attending that I would be like Frankenstein's monster when they were done.

"You're still you, Jane," one of the residents called out. I remember staring at her, that young and eager doctor in training, long after she'd finished interrupting. I wanted to catch the soft flesh of her earlobe in my teeth, feel the tickle of that light peach fuzz on each bud of my tongue.

My nurse then said that my parents and brother were waiting to see me and could they come in now? But I told her I was tired, so maybe later.

**

Now the surgery is over, and I am awake, looking at a face in the mirror they say is mine.

After waiting for my sobs to fill the room, the doctors leave upon seeing my anticlimactic reaction. I say, thank you, but I would just like to sleep.

My beautiful resident closes the door and stays inside. "You don't have to pretend to be so strong."

"I'm not pretending. I don't mind. I wasn't attached to the old face." I sound sure, and therefore I probably am.

She makes her way to my bedside. "Does it look very different?" She looks so sorry.

"Yes." I don't hesitate or dress the truth up prettier than it is.

"We do our best, but when the damage—" She talks in that sweet honey singsong I've enjoyed so much, even as it's made her colleagues roll their eyes when she speaks with confident authority. I stop her, though I like to listen to her. The music of her.

"You don't need to do that. I know. I'm not upset with you."

"It's my fault," she says, but I sense the words before I hear them. "I'm new at getting to assist during the procedures. And my hand—I got so nervous. It shook, and I'm so sorry."

She's breathing too fast for language to keep up, and I place my hand on hers—the one she indicated had been the guilty party during my surgery. I can feel it tremble now beneath mine. I reach for her arm, to pull her closer to me, until I feel the rigid tension in her small frame start to lessen, and then she's seated on my bed as I want.

"It's the only way you baby doctors can learn," I tell her with a smile I mean genuinely even if it looks false, like a stranger's. "Besides, they wouldn't have let you do anything too important."

She laughs with tears in the notes. "You're not the one supposed to be comforting me."

"Maybe. But you're upset, and I'm not. So this way makes sense for now, right?"

"What are you, a saint?" She notices the fixation of my eyes on her earlobes, and the mood in the room shifts. I know she'll probably leave any minute now, and I'll let her. Then it'll just be me and the mirror. Alone.

"Sad that being understanding and decent qualifies one for sainthood now," I say, but I keep my tone light and playful as I release her hand and readjust my body against the pillows behind me. I'm not looking at her anymore, and I think she knows she'd better go. She stands, and I focus on the wrinkles and creases of her turquoise scrubs so I can unmemorize her face.

"You're very nice to make me feel better, but I am still sorry," she says.

"You're forgiven."

She seems to be going and is almost gone. But then she turns around and leans back against the door and nods at me. Something in her expression reminds me of the warmth intermingled with pity that I could read in the faces of all my loved ones the first time they saw me after it happened. It was maybe not as painful as it would be if they'd physically recoiled, but somehow it felt like they had anyway. I haven't let any of them come back inside my room since before the surgery. I'm told they took turns showing up for a while, just in case, only to be rejected outside my door. Each day, my nurses would remind me that they were there, in the waiting room, poised and ready for when I'd change my mind. Until I didn't, and the nurses stopped saying they were there. I can't ask now, even though I wonder and need to know. Because what if they're not anymore? I hate my doctor for staying.

"Don't look at me."

She stares out the window instead. Then she waits until I start to cry. Once I do finally begin, it's hard to stop. I rub and scratch at my left earlobe so fiercely and savagely that my nails nearly draw blood. I don't know why I seek to destroy my own pacifier, but I want to claw my earlobes until they resemble the pulp of a blood orange, like I imagine my whole face did in the back of the ambulance that night. When she wrestles my hands away from my ears and hugs me, I almost ask—did any of them wait for me? Are they still here?

Sara's Someone

I was probably eight years old when I first began to suspect that Sara had invented me. I'd never had any reason to question my existence before.

I knew it was a bit rude that no one ever talked to me. They only talked to Sara. But I just figured that was a personality thing. You know, she's the talkative, approachable one. I'm the shy, quiet one.

Then it came to me that Sara had parents, teachers, classmates, but I didn't have any of my own. I was Sara's best friend. That part of my identity was rock solid still. But was I not also someone's daughter, someone's student, or any kind of someone without Sara?

I was too afraid to voice my suspicions to her. Would I lose the only friend I'd ever known? If I confronted her and was right, would she imagine me out of existence as easily as she'd willed me into being? So I kept it to myself and continued with our normal routine.

I wake up when Sara wakes up. I fall asleep when Sara falls asleep. I'm not sure what happens to me when we close our eyes and consciousness fades away. I don't dream or whatever like she does. When she tells me her fanciful or frightening stories in the morning, I just nod and listen, though I can't relate.

I brush my teeth when Sara brushes hers. My clothes are in Sara's closet. I compliment her on whatever outfit we've chosen for her to wear, but then we sort of forget to pick or comment on mine together. All of a sudden, I'm just wearing it, and neither she nor I seem to care what color it is or how it sits on my body. I know how I'd describe Sara's body if you were to ask me, but though I've stood in front of the mirror beside her day in and day out for years now, I'm a little bit fuzzy on what to tell you about me.

It makes sense that we focus on her of course. Sara wants to look nice so other people might admire, envy, or even develop a crush on her, but who is there for me to impress besides Sara? Hers is the only approval I've ever had in mind, and for a long time, she gave it to me freely. As we prepare to enter middle school, though, I can feel myself registering smaller and smaller on her scale of importance. My silent concerns morph into burning resentment. Even if she'd insult me, it might be better. But it's worse. She doesn't really have any opinion of me at all anymore.

My desperation and hurt seep into our every interaction. I overdo it, trying to recreate the magic of our past. I tug at her nostalgia too hard and too often until the words, remember when, are enough to spark her now default mode of impatience. I see the disinterest and distance in her eyes and I can't understand my inability to make her care again. On one particularly painful evening spent attempting and failing to earn her laughter—my favorite sound in the world—I look down at my hands and notice the faded, translucent quality to the left one. From the wrist down, it looks and feels impermanent. I flex my fingers or my mind tries to, but nothing happens.

Is it murder if you are erased by your own creator? What else should I call it?

If you're mad, I wish you'd just tell me, I say.

I'm not mad, she says.

What happened to us? I ask her this over and over. Waiting for a new answer.

I don't know. You're different, she tells me. Her tone becomes so bored by the hundredth time she has to say it, and I feel a twinge of guilt for the listless affect she now brings with her everywhere she goes—to the kitchen table with her parents, to the classroom, to time spent with her new friends.

Sara, you're different, they all start to tell her.

She seems depressed, the school counselor alerts her parents. Perhaps schedule a visit to a child psychologist.

Sara has never told anyone about me before, so I don't expect talking to this adult will be any different. But after a few agonizing sessions, Sara points at me. She's here, she says. She's always here.

To watch her reveal me to this stranger is somehow both a betrayal and relief.

I think it's time to let her go, the doctor says. I don't think you need her anymore.

I'm not entirely sure which one of us she's talking to.

Sara closes her eyes and nods. As I look down to see my own torso vanishing, I know that it's me who is no longer needed. I've been right all along. I'm not imagining it. Without Sara, I'm not a someone.

As I wait to disappear, float, dissolve or however it works into vapor or nothingness, I find I'm no longer in the office. But I'm not gone either. No, I'm in a field. The cornfield behind Sara's house that we loved to run around in together, chasing lightning bugs with our mason jars at the ready. It was our favorite place and activity until I told her I didn't think we should do it anymore. If I were a lightning bug, I wouldn't like it, I said. Trapped and slamming around against the insides of a cute little jar, my wings beating in a panicked frenzy. I worried she'd be mad, but she agreed with me. From then on, we ran around with the lightning bugs, not after them.

So maybe I won't go just yet. Maybe I'll stay here for a while in case she does ever need me again. Glowing bright and flying at her side.

Doors

When he shows it to me, the place where people go to start from scratch and pick the unopened door they skipped the last time—a do over, no questions asked—I am afraid.

"What's scary? It's an amazing opportunity," he says dismissively.

Technology makes something new possible every day. I should stop being so surprised at each astounding leap into unknown, irrevocably altered futures and instead celebrate the daily dissolving of boundaries blocking our path to happiness—but I'm a skeptic by nature.

"Only once?" I ask him. "Like you can't pick several points in your life, say, and try to redo all of them."

"Just the once." He is both firm and casual. "Wouldn't work otherwise. Time's all too interwoven and dependent, right?" He coughs out a puff of smoke, and I wonder if his door should be the one where he tried his first cigarette. If he'll open that other door, the one where his lungs are fresh and unburdened, and people don't glare at him huddled in building entryways underneath *No Smoking* signs on icy winter days, polluting their clean air. Feels a bit like he's wasting this monumental one-time deal on me. "Can't change one choice without changing everything that comes after it," he continues. "Nothing would be the same anymore anyway."

"True." I trace lazy scrawling shapes along the curve of his bare shoulder with the bones of my knuckles, eliciting a shiver on this hot as hell afternoon. "I guess I don't see how remorse wouldn't be inevitable. No matter which door you end up choosing—won't the other always hold an allure, the appeal, the romance of the one you can't have?"

He shrugs off my touch. We only get physical with each other after the break up when we're high, and I'm the one high right now. Not him. He points up at the two doors that I now notice are looming over us, ornate and majestic. He coughs again.

"Well?" I gesture at the doors. "Now what?"

"Now we decide," he says.

"Between the two?"

He rolls his eyes because we both know I'm just killing time, putting things off, and he's not going to explain it all again.

"I stood in line forever to make this happen," he says. "We agreed."

If we walk through the door he wants, then we were only ever friends. If we walk through that door, we never fell in love. Our current friendship would be unburdened by the too familiar intimacy and history we share. I'd be able to touch his shoulder without him flinching with regret and me longing for another try to get it right this time. I see the resolve in his expression. He's ready and willing to undo it all, everything he sees now only as complications—irritating rather than beautifully painful and revelatory.

"You really think this way is better?" I bob and weave, almost catching his eye but ultimately failing. "I don't mind that things are hard. I love you anyway."

He frowns at my feet. "Yeah. I want to be able to love you again, too. I can only do that if we're just friends again. That's it." I hear the guilt twang in that last note. "I'm doing this for us."

"Okay."

We move over to his desired door together. He opens it. I hope he'll change his mind, no matter how last minute. But no. I know him better than that. He's too confident and stubborn.

He takes my hand and closes his eyes. I wait for his body to go slack and peaceful.

Then I yank my hand out of his and place both of mine on his back. Before he can understand, speak, or resist, I shove him as hard as I can through the doorway. I remain behind.

When we meet somehow on the other side, he will be blissfully unaware and know only our friendship. I alone will know every gorgeous and uncomfortable moment we passed together as more than that.

I don't know. Ask me tomorrow if I made the right call.

Her Song

Perched on my rock, slippery and smooth beneath me, I can see them coming. A hazy mirage, blurry but massive, turned real in the distance. I call the sound, first from deep within my belly, and let it reverberate up my spine. It navigates the curves of my ribs and trills its way through the dark labyrinth of my esophagus until it scales the length of my throat and climbs into the reddest part of my mouth. Then I curl the notes up in my tongue before releasing my power. It's ticklish and pleasurable. This is part of why I wait and hold it there, feeling the next one build inside me like an unyielding wave. I do this all with the utmost sincerity. I don't wield my ability with any kind of boastful or cocky strut.

I free the song from its wet prison. The men on the approaching ship hear my music call to them for the first time. It blankets the sky above and ripples over the sea below, until I'm all they can see and all they can hear. My voice is a thing of beauty, my wordless charm arresting. They'll crash like the rest before them and descend into their new watery home. I will fill the cold, vast quiet with a melody that will make them love me, even as they sleep an endless night. My lullaby soothes, and then silence bathes us all. They'll hear me for eternity and know they are happy.

I don't sing because I am dangerous. I am dangerous because I sing.

Turmeric & Sugar

Bhavi's parents had long raised him on the bitter and sweet life has to offer by, each morning, scattering over the top of his head a mixture of the two. The fine grains and crystals of mustard colored turmeric and beige sugar were interwoven among the strands of his thick, dark hair like a comforting, invisible crown. "In this way," his mother had said, "today's difficulties will be lessened and overcome by its beauties."

And yet, he'd come home each evening with a new tale of woe. His locker at school had been decorated with toilet paper, his books found lurking in the cavernous depths of hallway trash cans, and his teacher had called him a "know-it-all" again for simply providing the correct answers to questions she'd posed to the whole class, including him.

"If she didn't want to know, why did she ask?" Bhavi fretted over dinner.

"It's not about you," his father said. "The problem is with her. Don't let her bother you."

"Maybe you're using too much turmeric, Mom," Bhavi said. "You're giving me only the bitter, not enough sugar."

"If I use too much, you'll get a toothache and grow to take it for granted or even dislike it." She stroked his hair with fingertips stained yellow from the guilty spice causing his misfortunes. "Take heart. There are always lovely little treasures buried in darkness." When he frowned, she kissed the tip of his nose. "It just makes it feel that much better when you find them," she said.

When Bhavi first saw Soo standing at the front of his second grade class, staring at her shoes and letting her black hair fall forward like a gleaming curtain to conceal her face, he didn't think much of it. *Hard to be the new girl mid-year* was all that briefly flitted between his oversized ears. But as she wound her way through the tight aisles to her empty desk two rows behind his, he started to pay attention. He saw her sidestep the outstretched foot of Billy Perkins with pride. He resisted the temptation to reach over and smack Billy for trying to trip her so soon on her first day. He thought of speaking up.

Then he realized she wasn't frightened of Billy. She was mad. Dark, red mad. Blood coursing through the fierce expression in her eyes. He loved it, and he felt his bones strengthen and harden in her presence. Her friendship would be the sugar he'd been waiting for, finally emerging to conquer all the turmeric. Bhavi's cold teacher, who often glowered at him like he was an unpleasant scent lodged in her flared nostrils, called out his name, and he turned to face the front, startled. He felt safe enough a few minutes later to glance back at Soo.

Seated at her desk, she looked up like she felt him looking. Her face was diamond shaped like home plate. The lids guarding her brown eyes were pink petals. It seemed others had tried to rob her of her shine, too, but he could still see it there—like his—a candle wavering in the dark winds of childhood, its flame not yet gone out. Ready to burst and scorch, as well as light up, the night.

Acknowledgments

"Mae and Me" was first published in *Catapult*.

"You Don't Have a Place Here" was first published in *OKD*.

"A Day for Watching Birds" was first published in *The Airgonaut*.

"Echo" was first published in *Jellyfish Review*.

"And There I'll Be" was first published in *Boston Accent Lit*.

"In Twenty Years" was first published in *Necessary Fiction*.

"The Suitor" was first published in *New Flash Fiction Review*.

"Rose Petals and Obligations" was first published in *Sea Foam Mag*.

"Ships in the Night" was first published in *Fiction Southeast*.

"How Then" was first published in *Pidgeonholes*.

"Nurture" was first published in *Berkeley Fiction Review*.

"Tape and Glue" was first published in *The MacGuffin*.

"Look Where We're Going" was first published in *X-R-A-Y*

"Long Distance Loyalty" was first published in *Riggwelter Press*.

"Tomorrow" was first published in *The Margins- AAWW*.

"You're Still You" was first published in *OKD*.

"Sara's Someone" was first published in *Wigleaf*.

"Doors" was first published in *HAD*.

"Her Song" was first published in *Fiction Southeast*.

"Turmeric & Sugar" was first published in *Little Fiction*.

Thank Yous

This book would not have been possible without the unwavering support of my parents, Ramani and Srinivas Vangala; my husband, Chi; our children, Liam and Dylan; and my brother, Ram. You all have my love and gratitude forever. Thank you as well to the many relatives and family friends who would immediately drop everything to read my work as soon as it was published—it meant everything to me as I was just starting out.

Many of the stories in this book were first written in classes taught by Charles Wyatt, Ben Loory, and Stephen Cooper. They then went on to grow and evolve in workshops led by Tananarive Due, Victoria Patterson, and Peter Selgin. I am deeply grateful to them as well as my friends and peers who also contributed to the development of these pieces—most notably: Dele Lowman, Alisha Escobedo, Catalina Witman, Andrea Auten, Eric Newman, Genevieve Kersten, Luis Garcia Romero, and Lauren Dostal.

Thank you to the wonderful authors who took the time to read my book and offer their generous reviews in advance of its publication. I admire them, so their kind words meant a great deal to me—Cathy Ulrich, Tara Isabel Zambrano, Melissa Ragsly, Ben Loory, and Tananarive Due.

This book found a home because of the many editors who took a chance on me when I was unknown in the literary world. I am grateful to all who have published my writing, but particularly for Eric and Genevieve who believed in me and my work even when I didn't; Aaron Burch whose creative submissions calls inspired me to write new pieces out of thin air or finally finish ones I'd forgotten; Jennifer Todhunter for helping me to transform a story into something better than it was when I sent it to her; Matt Ortile who brought my work to so many new readers; and Scott Garson who encouraged me to keep going until I got it right. Editing at the following literary journals and working with the incredible people on the masthead at these places contributed to strengthening my own writing, so I will forever appreciate my time at *Lunch Ticket*, *Split Lip Magazine*, and *Pidgeonholes*.

As a teacher myself, I know the impact that mine from my younger days had on me and my writing—how far it's come, where it's going, and what it still has yet to be. Thank you to those who saw something in both me and my voice so early on: Diane Afferton, Anne Dresser, Diane Downs, and Scott Eckstein.

Thank you to artist Carolyn Brandt for the beautiful and dreamy cover she created specifically for *Turmeric & Sugar*. It is better than anything I could have imagined.

Thank you to many more friends than I could ever hope to name for your endless support and encouragement of me and my writing over the years, but especially: Margaret Livingston, Michael Tapscott, Deepa Vasudevan, Cathy Fong, Lorena Hong, Mike Wilson, Suzy DiMont, Delilah Lora, Frances Trimyer, Vinesha Phillip-Civil, Jess Snow, Cynthia Abo, Cristina Medina, Patrick Garland, and Maria Chi.

To Josh Dale, Chanel Martins, and the whole Thirty West Publishing family: thank you for trusting me and my vision and for making a lifelong dream of mine come true.

This book—its very heart and soul—is for my Ammama. I wish you were here and that you'd been able to hold and read it yourself, but it wouldn't even exist if not for you. Thinking of and missing you always.

About the Author

Anna Vangala Jones is the author of the short story collection, *Turmeric & Sugar* (Thirty West Publishing, 2021). Her stories have been selected for Longform Fiction's Best of 2018 list and nominated for the Pushcart Prize and Best Small Fictions anthologies. Her fiction has appeared in *Catapult*, *Wigleaf*, and *Berkeley Fiction Review*, among others. Visit her online at annavangalajones.com